Ken Lansdowne

A **MYSTERY**

WRAPPED IN A **MYSTERY**

SURROUNDED BY A **MYSTERY**

A Bent Mystery
6

H Publishing

Publisher: H Publishing
605 Clinton Street,
Denver, Colorado 80247.

First Printing: 2013

Library of Congress Cataloging in Publication Data
    A Mystery Wrapped In A Mystery Surrounded By A Mystery : A Bent Mystery: a novel/ Ken Lansdowne
        p. cm.
    ISBN: 978-0-9740853-6-4
    1. Title

H Publishing

Printed in USA

BOOKS BY THE AUTHOR

Jacob Marley
A Gay Victorian Christmas Novella

THE BENT MYSTERY SERIES:
Secrets Don't Belong In Closets
A Murderous Ball Of Fluff
The Fairy Dust Killer
Home Sweet Homo
Dance:Ten Murder:Maybe?
A Mystery, Wrapped In A Mystery,
Surrounded By A Mystery

AUTHORS NOTE:

An issue has come up often enough that I feel I should address it and perhaps clarify it for you, the reader. The question has been asked if I am writing about 1986/1987 New York City or the present.

I write about 1980's New York because I know 1980's New York. It is the era I lived in the city. I know the streets, the stores, the neighborhoods. I don't know present day New York. Unfortunately, I have not returned to the city for a long time.

So, I am writing in these stories, as all writers are advised, about what I know. When I describe a street or a business on one of the streets it is because I know it was there. For instance, *Boots and Saddles*, a gay bar located on Christopher Street was then located in the building next to Village Cigars. As of 2008 Village Cigars was still there, but Boots had disappeared and was then a Jumba Juice. I have no idea what may be there in 2013. Sometimes, I have to admit, I will describe a place that is completely out of my imagination. For example, in *The Fairy Dust Killer* much of the action takes place in a gay bar and club called Cherries. This place has never existed. It is, in my mind, a combination of *Marie's Crisis*, *Don't Tell Mama's*, and *The Duplex*, three actual show bars in the area, with my own embellishments for the expediency of the novel. So the place is true to the spirit of the bars that existed then but totally cut from a writers fabric.

Now, to the issue of the technology I have used in the novels. I have tried to be correct and true to the period in this. Cell phones, which I do have my characters use, did exist in 1986 and 1987.

In fact they were introduced to the American public by Motorola in 1983. They were big—about the size and shape of a building brick—heavy—they weighed around 2 1/2 pounds—and expensive—$3,995.00 in 1980's money—but they were available. So I have my people use them legitimately. Len Matthews is a successful Broadway actor and could certainly afford to own such a device. Also available by 1987 were CD's, VCR's(in both Beta and VHS formats), cable TV, and personal computers. I have JB using a PC—introduced in 1981—in these stories. He is, after all, a known writer who could use the latest machines for his writing. Admittedly, most computers in the 80's were used by business and would usually require an entire floor and frigid temperatures to keep the servers running. And the PC's that were available to the general public were primarily word processors with rudimentary spreadsheet capabilities. There was no internet, games were of the ping pong ball skidding back and forth on a black screen variety, but computers for home use were coming into their own in the time of the novels.

What I am saying is that I try to keep the books true to the period they take place in, and hope that these issues are now clarified and will add to the pleasure you take in the reading of them. Thanks for letting me have my say...

Ken Lansdowne

A **MYSTERY**

WRAPPED IN A **MYSTERY**

SURROUNDED BY A **MYSTERY**

CHAPTER 1

Insistent.

It was the only word to describe the phone while JB was right in the middle of working his way over a particularly difficult hump on his latest novel.

Sometimes, for a writer, the right words take a bit of time to get from that place in the brain where creative happens. That was exactly the case for

JB right that moment. He had been at it for a few hours by then. Trying this series of words, hating the combination, erasing them from the screen of his computer, trying again with a different set of words, erasing, trying, erasing...

Finally, after staring at the wall for several minutes, JB had come up with what he was thinking was just the right set of words to transition into the next phase of the chapter. He was typing this inspiration when the phone began jangling at him. Not wanting to disturb the flow, he let the answering machine get the annoying instrument.

Jeremy Bent, or JB to all his acquaintances, was a reasonably successful mystery novelist and part-time Broadway theatrical writer. Hovering in his early forties he was tall, slim, and still clinging to damned attractive. An unapologetic gay man he had managed to break through the lavender ceiling and have his work, several popular mystery novels, accepted by mainstream publishers and critics. He'd also written a play that had been produced with a short run on Broadway, and had dabbled in television early in his career. He made his living writing. His avocation was sticking his nose into various police matters and mysteries up to and including murders. Although it made the cops he dealt with mad as hatters, his dillydallying in their cases had provided him with the plots for his last five novels. Avocation or vocation? Tomatoes/Potato's? It couldn't be all bad if it produced, now could it?

It was late afternoon on a chilly February day in New York City. Two months into Nineteen-eighty-seven. The machine had already picked up two other messages. Once he was finished with the transition he was working on and was at a reasonable stopping point he would go and see what his callers had left on the machine for him.

The first two calls weren't of any importance—an insurance salesman and he'd won a free weekend in the Pocono's if he would listen to an all-day solicitation for a time-share. Not very likely. He deleted them both. The third message, however, caught his immediate interest.

It was left by Chad Easterly, a friend of his who worked in the GMHC offices down in the Village.

Chad was a counselor at the Gay Men's Health Crisis HIV testing clinic. Located on the second floor of the Gay Community Center in Greenwich Village, the clinic was a place where gay men could go to be anonymously tested for the HIV virus, the precursor to AIDS. If they tested positive then Chad was the one who would be talking with them, soothing these distressed young men who had received the crippling diagnosis.

JB knew Chad because he was a volunteer with the GMHC's Buddy program. This was a group of gay men who would look after one of these ailing men when they became too ill to do for themselves.

After the death of Liberace from AIDS eariler that week—despite his people's protestations that it was complications from a watermelon diet that had killed him—JB assumed that Chad was calling with a new assignment for JB to take on. The clinic always got busier when the disease was mentioned in the papers or someone famous died. Chad probably had a new man who needed the bit of care that JB might be able to provide. Sometimes cleaning a sick man's apartment, or walking his dog, or buying groceries, or doing the laundry, went a long way to making a compromised life more bearable. JB was glad to do any or all of those things for these men who needed what help he could give.

But Chad's message wasn't saying he had someone new for JB to look after. He was saying that he wanted JB to come into the clinic to meet someone. Someone who he thought JB needed to see. Someone he would be interested in. That was different. And intriguing.

JB checked his watch. It was still early, he could get down to the West Village from his East Sixty-fourth Street apartment in about forty-five minutes. He grabbed his coat, locked up, and walked to the subway.

CHAPTER 2

The Gay Community Center was in the old Food and Maritime Trades High School on West Thirteenth Street between Seventh and Eighth Avenue's. It had been taken over and become the gay center in Nineteen-eighty-three. Since it's opening it was a place where the gay men and women of New York City could come and meet, dance, and be. It also provided necessary services to the community such as HIV testing and counseling.

JB went up the stairs to the clinic and went in. The reception desk was unmanned at the moment and there were only two men sitting in the double row of metal chairs over on the left. He headed to the back of the room where there were several desks protected by a wall of grey metal filing cabinets.

Chad was sitting at his desk talking with another man. He looked up at JB, acknowledged him, and indicated he would be only a moment. JB stood and waited. While he did he studied the posters tacked up on the wall opposite him. Most were advocating the use of condoms to prevent the spread of AIDS. Good advice given in simple graphic terms.

Behind the wall was a warren of examining rooms and offices where the main business of the clinic took place. Blood taking, private rooms to talk with patients—the heart of the clinic.

Chad finished with the man at his desk and they stood. Chad was a young man of about twenty-five. Longish brown hair cut haphazardly, attractive with a preppy sort of style, active dark eyes, and a friendly smile. He shook hands with the man he was talking to and walked him to the aisleway where JB was standing. The man said thank you and then left. Chad turned to JB.

"I'm glad you could get here, JB. We have someone here who I think you will be fascinated by." He took hold of JB's arm and guided him over to the doorway to the back rooms. "This guy is really out of our bailiwick. We called Bellevue, but they can't fit him in until tomorrow. You know we're connected with Bellevue Hospital so they would normally handle this sort of thing. But they don't have anything for tonight. That's where you come in."

"Hold on. Don't you think we should discuss this for a minute. Then you could explain what the hell you're talking about. I'd feel a lot better if I knew what was going on."

"Of course. You're absolutely right. Come on, sit here." He indicated a row of chairs along the hallway wall facing the doors to the examining rooms. He sat next to JB and began. "You know what we deal with here in the clinic, JB. Men who are anxious and worried if they might be sick or not. Well, that isn't what we have here."

"What do you have?" JB raised his eyebrows in question.

"This morning, when the receptionist came in to open, he found this strange man sitting on the steps by the main doors downstairs. He was disoriented and had a bad gash on his forehead. From some sort of beating he'd taken. Mugged in the Village last night was our guess. Jerry—that's the receptionist—is studying to be a nurse, so he brought the guy upstairs here and took care of the wound. Turned out it wasn't deep and didn't look really serious, but Jerry, while he talked to the guy, discovered something odd."

"Odd? So what already?"

"He discovered that the guy has no memory. He has no idea what happened to him. Nothing. Jerry gave him some aspirin and then called me. I hightailed it down here and we've spent the day trying to help the poor guy. To be honest its been a sort of relief. I spend most of my time here taking with distraught men who think they're going to die. This has been, to say the least, more diverting. I'm not a doctor, but I think this guy has a case of retrograde amnesia. He's lost all memory of his recent past. He doesn't even know his name. He can't remember what happened to him last night. Where he lives is a total blank."

"Wait a minute. Are you sure this isn't just some guy having an alcoholic blackout. I have a friend that used to have those before he quit drinking."

"No, that isn't it. He's completely sober. And a blackout wouldn't make him forget his own name, or where he lives. It wouldn't wipe out his entire identity."

"That's true. Then how far back does he remember? Does he have any memories from his past at all? Last week? The day before? How severe is it?"

"That's what we've been trying to figure out. Aric—that's what we've been calling him—has been mostly in shock, and not very forthcoming with much information."

"Understandable, under the circumstances."

"When we couldn't get him into Bellevue and realized there wasn't any place for him to stay I thought of you. I knew you would be interested in seeing a real case of amnesia. And you have that big apartment. I thought maybe you could help him. What do you say?"

"I say why haven't you called the police? They should have been called right away, don't you think?"

"The police? What would they do? JB, this guy is scared out of his wits. He's totally alone and frightened of his own shadow at this point. If the cops showed up he'd be even more traumatized. Can you imagine what a basketcase he'd be after a night in a jail cell? Listen, JB, the doctors at Bellevue can help him. Just not until tomorrow when the clinics there open. He has an appointment at nine. I just don't know what to do with him tonight. There's no place for him. I haven't got room. I live in a tiny studio. He can't stay here overnight. I thought with your mystery writing background you would be really interested in meeting with this guy. And maybe helping him? Aren't you interested? Come on, say you are. I know you. And I know you'll like him. At least talk to him."

"Well, I can do that, I suppose."

And it was at that exact point where JB took the step that pulled him into a morass of trouble like he'd never seen before. If he'd only known....

"Good. Come on, he's right in here."

Chad got up and went to the doorway opposite where they had been sitting and opened the door.

In normal circumstances the man would have been considered very handsome. In his mid thirties—thirty-three or possibly thirty-five. But he seemed younger somehow. Almost boyish in his manner. Dark with an obvious Italian ancestry, heavy lashed eyes, full mouth, firm jaw, round cheeks. A square shaped, well built, gym body tapering to narrow hips and thighs. Attractive? Sure. A turn-on for many, but not really JB's type. There was a large white bandage wrapped about his head, a blood seepage mark where the wound was on his forehead. He was sitting on a medical bench and was looking mostly anxious and bemused right then. In need of care. He looked up at Chad and gave a weak smile.

"Aric, this is Jeremy Bent. The man I was telling you about. You remember?"

He nodded and held out his hand. JB took it and felt a strong grip. He looked into the man's eyes. They were filled with questions. Not surprising, considering what had happened. Also there was an eagerness there. A desire to help. Almost kid like and sweet in its sincerity. It brought out a nurturing aspect in JB he didn't even suspect he had.

"Call me JB. Everybody does."

"JB? That's the initials on my watch. Look." He slipped off the expandable band on an expensive looking gold watch he was wearing. He held it out.

JB took it and looked. Engraved on the back were the initials J and B in an Old English script. "Do you know who these initials are for?"

Aric shook his head. "I have no idea. But I had the watch on this morning. Maybe it's yours? The same initials, right?"

"Well, considering we just met I tend to doubt it. It's a very nice watch though." He handed it back. "So, maybe we can talk for a minute or two? Get to know each other?"

"I'm not so sure I can do that. I don't know much about myself."

"Maybe the three of us can piece a few things together. How about that?"

He nodded and put his hands in his lap, the same as a schoolboy in front of a teacher.

Well, he has manners, JB was thinking. He doesn't appear to be a brute or a hoodlum. That doesn't rule out thief or con-man though. "Chad called you Eric. Is that your name?"

"I don't know..."

"We've been calling him that because of this." Chad held out a leather coat. "He was wearing it when he got here, and he doesn't have any other identification. No wallet. Or any thing else to identify him. The name is Aric, with an A. It's the name on the label inside the coat." He shrugged. "It gave us something to call him."

JB took the coat and looked it over. It was long, cut like a trenchcoat or a duster, and made from a butter soft brown leather. Sensuous to the touch it draped languidly in JB's hands. It was in excellent condition, worn but not shabby. The leather sleeves had taken on the wear wrinkles of regular use at the bend of the elbows. It had a rounded collar without notches and decorative stitching in black as embellishment. There was a loose belt at the waist. JB realized right away that it wasn't something off of any department store rack. It had to be a custom piece. He checked the label on the inside. Stitched at the back collar it had the name *Aric* woven on a rectangle of cloth. This was from a professional, not something made as a one-off. The maker might have a shop he sells from here in New York.

And there it was. JB was once again being sucked, not necessarily screaming, into the problems of somebody else. His "have to help the troubled soul" genes were kicking into gear. He had another case to work out.

"Aric might be the name of the craftsman who made this. This isn't a standard leather coat. It looks like it was made by hand. But Aric is as good a name as any, I suppose. Do you like it?"

The man shrugged. "It's better than Oswald. Or Bertram." He smiled, showing the dimples on each cheek.

"You have a point. Then Aric it will be." JB held out the coat. "Is this yours then? Here, try it on." Aric stood, took the garment from JB, and wriggled into it.

"Bend your arms." JB leaned in. "Yep, it looks like the folds in the leather fit your shape. So the coat is probably yours. It isn't something you just picked up in a back alley somewhere."

Aric took it off and held on to it as he sat back down. "Then I must have some money. This isn't a cheap coat is it?"

JB shrugged. "Custom made. Expensive leather. You're right. Not a cheap garment. But it could have been given to you. Or bought at a really good sale. A thrift shop maybe? What do you remember, Aric? Anything?"

"I know what's happened since this morning. And that's about all."

"Nothing from before? What happened last night? How you got the gash on your head?"

"No. Nothing before this morning when Jerry found me on the steps of this building. And then meeting Chad, and now you."

"And everything before that is a blank?"

Aric nodded.

"What about when you were young? Do you remember being a child?"

He started to shake his head, then stopped. "Wait, I do remember something. I was in Canada when I was little. Until I was a teenager. Ottawa? Mother and Dad were there, I think, for his job. He was in the government. Ours not theirs. A lawyer maybe? But I was born in the States. In Maine? I don't know, it's all fuzzy."

Chad spoke up. "That's what's called memory recall. It's the mind accessing information you've experienced from your memory banks. Its like a big file cabinet inside there. You pull out a file and review the information. It will come at you like that. In fragments. It's normal."

"Well, at least something about me is normal. This is so weird. Not knowing. It's making me crazy."

JB spoke in as soothing a voice as he could. "Aric, you've had a major blow to the head. It's scrambled some of the receptors inside there. You know, it could all come back tomorrow. What you need is to get some rest. I think you should come home with me, get a good night's sleep, and then we'll get you to the doctors over at Bellevue tomorrow. That sounds like a good idea, right?"

Chad rang in with the same recommendation and Aric agreed. They gathered his few belongings—his coat and shoes, his watch, and they left the center together.

Once out on the street JB realized he hadn't eaten since that morning. He'd skipped lunch. "Are you hungry, Aric? Did they give you anything to eat while you were at the clinic?"

"I had half a sandwich and iced tea at eleven. Jerry shared his sack lunch with me."

"Then you must be hungry. Let's go over to One Potato. It's close. At Houston and Tenth. We can have dinner there."

"But I don't have any money." He reached into his jeans pockets and pulled them out. He shrugged.

JB noticed Aric was wearing a pair of *Levi* button fly jeans. They ran about thirty-five dollars a pair. And practically every gay man in the Village owned them. Maybe Aric was right when he'd said he must have money. His shirt was a cotton plaid from Bill Blass, again not cheap. His sneakers were *Rebock's*. They were trendy and probably cost in the eighty to one hundred dollar range. The watch was an expensive gold affair that seemed heavy and old fashioned for the upwardly mobile younger set that Aric appeared to belong too. Yuppies they were being called, and Aric was probably a member of the club.

"Not to worry. I'll take care of it," JB said. They started walking over to the cafe. "By the way, Aric, if anything should look familiar to you don't hesitate to tell me. There might be some reason you ended up at the center this morning. Maybe it was a familiar place to you? Do you think you're gay? You're clothes could indicate that you might be."

"Do they? I don't know. Nothing has hit me as familiar so far."

"Well, how about some word associations? That might point to whether you're gay or straight. Does the word fuchsia make you think of a color or a pasta?"

"Your joking aren't you? But am I gay?" Aric stopped walking and stood on the street, thinking. Trying to access some memory locked away in his head. JB watched as he struggled. As he was about to tell him that it wasn't a problem, to come on to the restaurant, Aric spoke up.

"Its like a slide show inside. Images slipping past. I'm naked...in a shower. A communal shower, like a high school gym, or a barracks. There's a man with me. There's only the two of us though. He turns toward me and grabs his privates. I can't look away..."

"How old are you in this scene? A child? A teenager? An adult? I ask because it makes a difference. A teenager can get turned-on by a J.C. Penny catalog, so his real sexuality has little bearing. Adults it takes a bit more."

"I'm grown. I get a hard-on too."

"Probably you're gay then."

"The man's familiar. Blond. Tall. Good-looking. A friend?"

"Someone from your past I guess."

Aric's hand went to his head and rubbed. "There's more. Another place. Eariler? Or maybe later. This time it's a woman. She's Asian...and naked too. On a bed. And another. Another woman I mean. She's not Asian. With long dark hair. She's standing. And she's naked too. What does it mean?"

"Maybe you're bisexual, Aric. Attraction has all kinds of avenues and byways."

"Then I still don't know if I'm gay."

"I doesn't matter. Gay. Straight. Whatever. We'll figure out what's happened and it will all be cleared up. Give it some time."

Aric grabbed at his head, again rubbing at his temples.

"Are you all right?, JB asked.

"My head. It's hurting."

"Then stop for now. Let's get some food." They continued their walk.

As they went along JB was putting a few ideas in

a row. Aric still had his watch, expensive from the looks of it, so robbery probably wasn't the reason for the head injury he'd suffered. But he had no money, or identification, or wallet. So where was he from? And what was with him walking around the Village all night? Better yet, why had he stopped at the gay community center that morning? It could be there was some dim memory at work that had led him to a place he knew. Or had he just sat on those particular steps out of fatigue? What had happened to cause his amnesia? Who had cracked open his skull, and then left him to wander in what had to be, in his condition, unfamiliar territories? Hell, even JB could get turned around and lost in the melange of streets and alleys that made up Greenwich Village. There was a lot that JB needed to figure out if he had any chance at all of helping this young man.

One Potato was actually a bar with a few tables off to the side for sitting at while you ate. JB and Aric took their seats and looked at the menu chalked on a large blackboard hanging against the back wall. When the waiter showed up JB ordered a cheeseburger with fries. Aric ordered a hamburger also, but insisted that it be cooked rare, no onions or pickles, with cheddar cheese not American, and with the mustard on the side. Also the fries had to be crisp.

"That's very specific, Aric. Where did that come from?"

"I don't know. But it sort of came out. Natural like."

"It must be the way you always order your burgers. It's a reflective action. A learned response to the food ordering process. So there are some memory synapses at work inside your head."

"That's a good sign, isn't it? Maybe you were right. It will all come back."

"Let's hope so. What I'd like to do right now is delve some more into your early life. You seemed to have some lingering memories of that. So let me ask a few more questions. I might jog something loose. Are you up for it? Is your head feeling all right?"

"Sure. Anything that might get this clear..."

It turned out that Aric did have some scattered memories up to the time he went off to college. But he didn't know what school he'd gone to. He remembered being a teenager in Yonkers, New York, after Canada. He knew he went to both public and prep schools, but couldn't name them. He lost his parents to a car accident when he was still a teen. Bits and pieces came back. He'd studied architecture, but didn't think he worked as an architect. He lived in New York City, but had no clue where. There was a miasma of random facts running around in his head. He just couldn't put all the pieces together to make them into a complete picture.

When they'd finished their meal JB led Aric over to West Street. He wanted to stop at *The Leather Chest*, a boutique shop there in the Village. He had dealt with the owner and was thinking it would be a good idea to show him the coat that Aric was wearing.

CHAPTER 3

Stitcher Rumsey was the owner, salesman, craftsman, and all around everything of *The Leather Chest.* His stock in trade was supplying the gay S&M crowd with the necessary accessories for their particular pleasures. On display in the shop were slings, chaps, vests, barracks hats, jackets, wristbands and rings, paddles, whips...You name it—if it was made of leather then Stitcher carried it.

When JB and Aric stepped in, Stitcher—a huge man who looked like a miscreant thug with short prison chopped hair and a mean scar on his cheek—was busy fitting a pair of open assed chaps on a customer. Actually Stitcher was a sweetheart who loved working with his chosen material and got the scar from the errant claw of one of the many cats he kept around the store. He looked up, waved and sent the man he was working with off to the dressing room.

He stood and came over to JB, grabbed him in a bear hug, and kissed his cheek. "So good to see you, darling. It's been too long." He looked over at Aric. "And who's this. A new boyfriend?"

"Nothing of the sort. He's a new friend. Just a friend."

"You can never have too many of those. What can I do for you today?"

"I was wondering if you could look at this coat and see if you know the maker. Nobody knows the leather scene here in New York better than you."

Aric took off his coat and handed it over. Stitcher took it and began to examine it. "Humm. Good work. Definitely not a novice." He looked at the label. "Aric. The name is familiar. But where?" He thought a moment. "Oh, I know. Last year... No, it was the year before. At the FIT student fashion show. This Aric showed a pair of leather pants and a matching jacket. It was too die for. I was jealous, let me tell you. Maybe he's opened a shop somewhere here in the city. You should go over to the school. They might be able to tell you."

JB thanked him for the information and they left the store, walked up to Christopher Street, turned, and headed for the Avenue. The number One line subway station was at Sheridan Square.

As they walked up the street they wove past pairs and groups of gay guys out for walks or for cruising. They passed a small crowd gathered in the doorway of Ty's and spilling out of the Triangle. Over the din of the patrons boisterous chatter music wafted out to the street from thumping sound systems inside the bars. As they got closer to the Avenue they passed by Boots & Saddles. That's when Aric said, "JB, you said I should say something if anything was familiar."

"That's right. What is it?"

"That song. *What Am I Gonna Do About You?*" From in there." He pointed over at Boots. "It's Reba's newest. Reba McEntire. The singer."

Really? As they had walked up the street they had heard snatches from all the latest hits. *"Walk Like An Egyptian"*, *"True Colors"*, even *"Papa Don't Preach"*. And what he recognized was a country western song by Reba McEntire? This was getting strange. Weird even.

They crossed the Avenue and went down the stairs into the subway station. First stopping at the booth where JB purchased tokens, they went through the turnstiles and waited on the platform for the next train. One roared in within minutes and they caught an express to Grand Central Station. Once there they walked up a set of concrete stairs and then over to the platform for the Number Six Lexington Avenue line. That train got them in the vicinity of East Sixty-fourth Street and JB's apartment building.

Aric had followed JB docilely during all this without making comment, just keeping close to him so as not to lose him in the crowds rushing everywhere through the underground system. As they got back above ground and were walking toward JB's building, JB asked, "So did any of that ride ring any bells for you? In the subway? The lines we were on? The One or the Six? Maybe you use them to get to work. Most New Yorkers do."

"It was all so confusing. It was familiar, in the sense that I know I've been on the subway before. But not so I'd know a station to get off at. I just followed you."

"Okay. That's all right. We'll get you to my place and you can rest tonight. Then tomorrow we'll make sure you get to your appointment at Bellevue. They may have some answers for you. This is my place."

They went to the door. JB fished his keys from the loop at his back pocket and he opened the lobby door. He stepped aside for Aric and then went in after him. That's when he saw Len sitting on the floor by his door, with his head slumped on his knees and sound asleep.

Len Matthews was an ex-lover who had stayed around and become his best friend. He was also only about nine or ten months sober in Alcholics Anonymous. Asleep in a hallway wasn't a good sign.

CHAPTER 4

It took JB only a moment to go over and kick at Len's shoe.

He started and looked up. "What? Oh, JB, its you. I wanted to see you." He shook his head and then struggled to stand. JB reached out, took his wrist, and pulled him up. Although Len didn't smell of booze he had just had a slip a few months before, so JB had to ask. "Tell me you haven't been drinking, please."

"Good God, no." Len swiped at his ass with his hands. Then he looked over at Aric. "And ix-nay in front of the anger-stray. There's a reason its anonymous. I was just tired, and I fell asleep while I was waiting for you. No big deal. I told you I was done with all that. Don't you believe me?"

"Not a stranger, a new friend. And this isn't the first time I've found you passed out in the lobby of an apartment building, or even the fountain in front of the Plaza. So its a logical question."

"Okay. I guess you have a point. My past does bite me in the ass far too often. But I hope you'll learn to trust me. I intend to stay clean this time. Believe me."

"I want to, Len. Why aren't you at the theater?"

"It's Monday. It's dark tonight. So, It's my night off." Len Matthews was a well known actor, currently playing the male lead in a musical on Broadway. "So, I went to a meeting. That's why I wanted to talk to you." Len had joined AA almost a year before and had started to straighten out his life, if one of the most out gay actors in New York City could be said to do anything close to straight. His underwear didn't have skid marks, they had glitter streaks.

JB was putting the key into his door. "Well, come on in then. Do you want anything?"

"Just an introduction..." Len gestured toward Aric, who had followed them inside.

"Oh, sorry. This is Aric. He's a friend I met at the clinic down in the Village. Chad called me to come down."

Len shook Aric's hand and then waited while JB made him comfortable. He told him to sit, then offered a glass of something—Soda? Tea? Coffee?

Aric declined and said, "You know what. I'm

really tired. More than I thought I was."

"Okay, I'll change the sheets in the bedroom and you can sleep in there."

"I can't take your bedroom, JB. Why don't I sleep here? On the couch. That would be fine."

"Its really not a problem. I have a pull-out sofa in my office. I can sleep there."

"No..." Aric stretched out on the couch and pulled a pillow under his head. "Seriously, this is fine." He yawned. "I'll just stay here."

"Then let me get you a blanket."

Len followed JB to the linen cabinet in the hall. "Another of your stray puppies, JB? You are truly incorrigible."

"Its nothing like that. I can explain. Go to the kitchen. I'll be only a minute."

JB carried the blanket out to the couch and found that Aric was already asleep.

He covered him and went into the kitchen. Len handed him a cup of microwaved hot tea, and he sat at the table. He began to explain to Len what had led the young man to be sleeping on his sofa.

"Then he has no memory, JB? I noticed the bandage on his forehead. Is that why?"

"Probably. A blow to the head can be the cause of amnesia."

"Well, what are you going to do?"

"He has an appointment at Bellevue tomorrow morning. While he's there I thought I would go over to FIT."

"The Fashion Institute? Why?"

"His coat. It was designed by a student there. I want to track him down, see if he might remember Aric as one of his customers."

"You might be better off taking that watch he's wearing to a jeweler. I noticed it earler. Its old, JB. I'll bet its an heirloom. Maybe it could lead to his family."

"Very good, Len. That's an excellent idea. You're turning into quite the detective."

"Comes from hanging around you too much. I'm even beginning to like Miss Marple tweed. You know, I don't have to be at the theatre until late tomorrow. I could take the watch to someone."

"You would do that?"

"Sure. If you'll help me with something that happened today."

"What?"

"Well, with my schedule you know I haven't been able to get to a regular AA meeting. So I've been calling the hotline and going to the next meeting I could find when I have the time. Today I went to a closed meeting here on the Eastside. A real old-timers gathering. I had the least amount of time of anyone there, except for this one other guy."

"Wait, what's a closed meeting?"

"Oh, only members are allowed. Not like an anniversary meeting where friends and relatives are welcome."

"Okay. So what happened?"

"It wasn't a huge meeting. There were only about twelve people in this narrow room. It was the usual. A guy qualified. He had six years and told his story. Then he opened it up for sharing. That's another reason I've been going to different meetings. I've gotten tired of hearing the same people whine and complain about the same things week after week. At least I hear different people this way."

"Did you share? Its supposed to be good for you."

"No, not this time. As I said I had the least amount of sobriety. They didn't want to hear my newbie stuff."

"I'll bet they did. They're probably just as bored with their sharing as you said you were."

"They weren't bored today. I can tell you that."

"Why?"

"I said there was this other man there. The one who had even less time than I do. He only had a day or two. So, he held up his hand and got called. He said his name. I won't say it because its supposed to be anonymous, but it rhymes with Wick. And then he shared the damnest bunch of stuff you've ever heard, JB."

"What did he say?"

"You know this isn't supposed to be talked about, but its simply too kooky not to say something. First he said he was only a few days sober, and a mess. Well, that's not so unusual is it? But then he said it wasn't from not drinking. He knew he couldn't do that. And he hadn't. But he was freaked from having to do his job sober. He said it was the first time he'd done it without being stoned or drunk and it was really twisting him up."

"His job?"

"JB, you're not going to believe this, but he said he was a professional hitman. A hired killer. He kills people for a living. Can you believe it?"

"Did you believe it?"

"I don't know. Maybe. That's why I'm talking with you." Len went on telling what had happened. "You can bet saying what he said got everyone's attention. There wasn't a eye in the place that wasn't on him. He went on to share he had carried out a job the day before and it was weighing real heavy on him. He'd never felt guilty before about what he did. He actually said the people he 'offed'—That's the word he used—deserved what they got, but this time it was really bothering him. He was a wreak, and he was afraid he'd start drinking again."

"Did he say who he'd killed?"

"Not specifically. No names anyway. He said it was a woman, dark haired, who lived out in Westchester County. In Yonkers. He said she had a dark mole on her cheek and was real thin, almost scrawny. She lived in this big old Victorian kind of house. Painted white with green trim, with a widows walk on the third story. She was on it when he shot her with a high powered rifle. A single shot to the head."

Aric appeared in the kitchen doorway. "JB, help me. I think I'm having a heart attack. I can't breath...."

And he fell to the floor, pulled himself into a ball, and began to heave, trying to grab any air he could. JB was up and over to him in moments.

"Len, get him some water. Aric, it'll be all right. Are you having pains in your arm?"

"No, but my heart's going so fast. It's going to pound out of my chest. Help me."

JB took the glass of water and held it to Aric's lips. "Drink this. It'll help." He wrapped his arms around Aric and held him to his own chest. "Try to calm yourself. You'll be okay. I think you're having an anxiety attack. You've had a pretty shocking day. This is probably a reaction. Calm down, now."

It took him a few moments, but he did finally calm himself way down. He was still breathing heavily, but he wasn't so scared. "I was lying there on the couch, and I could hear you two talking in here. Suddenly, I couldn't get any air. And my chest was hurting. I was sweating. I knew I was going to die..."

"Len, in the bathroom. There's a prescription bottle of Valium in the medicine cabinet. Will you get me a couple?"

He left them while JB helped Aric get back to the couch. He lay back down and pulled the blanket up to his chin. "I don't get it. What happened?"

"You had a panic attack. It's over now. You'll take a couple of pills and go back to sleep. We can tell the doctors about this tomorrow." Len returned with the bottle. "Now take these. They'll help." He handed over two of the tablets. "Go to sleep, now."

JB and Len went back into the kitchen.

"Is he going to be all right?"

"I think so. He'll get checked out at the hospital and we'll know more." He picked up his cup and took a sip of his tea. "Why don't we go into my office. We can talk better in there and we won't disturb Aric." They moved into the other room, shutting the door behind them. "Now, back to this man at your meeting. Are you sure it wasn't just some delusional crazy spouting off?"

"That's kind of what I was thinking at first. We do get our share of wackos at meetings. That was until I found this at the newsstand in Grand Central." He handed over a copy of the *Yonkers Star,* a local paper for that area. It was that days issue and Len had folded it to an inside page.

Len pointed to an article that told of the mysterious shooting death of a local woman, a Miss Rosalie Stymington, at her home the day before. She had died from a single gunshot to the head. The accompanying picture showed a thin dark haired woman with a mole on her cheek.

"I think this is real, JB. The guy wasn't fooling."

"Well, what do you want me to do?"

"Well, this is just your kind of thing isn't it? A mystery to follow? You get to be Nancy Drew again."

"Since Nancy Drew never lost a case I'll take it you meant that as a compliment."

"We need to find this guy, JB—and turn him over to the police. He's a killer. A certified murderer."

"And no one stopped him at the meeting?'

"No. In fact, he left right after he shared. He got up, put on his coat, and walked out before the meeting was over."

"And how do you expect to find him then, Len? You said it was a closed anonymous meeting. How would we go about finding this guy? Could you even identify him?"

"I don't know. I was hoping you would have some ideas. Identify him? I suppose I would know him if I saw him again. He wasn't bad looking. Actually he was quite handsome. About thirty-five. Hunky. Hot, I guess, to a certain segment of the population. Of which I am a board certified member. Butch bruiser has always been my type."

"Well that's a start. I said I was going to FIT tomorrow. When I'm there I'll try to find an artist."

"To do what? Paint a mural? Then again, your place could use some sprucing up."

"Someone who you can give a description of this guy too and he can make a sketch. At least then we'll have an idea of who we're looking for. That might give us a beginning."

CHAPTER 5

The next morning JB was awake at four-thirty AM and couldn't get back to sleep. So he tip-toed past Aric, still asleep on the couch, and went into his office.

It took only moments for the computer to warm up and he picked up where he had left off the day before on his latest novel. Writing was soothing for JB. It was where he had complete control. Where everything was logical and had a reason for happening. Life on the other hand, with all its unhappy twists and turns, was often out of his reach. Like most everyone else JB was only able to keep his head above water and dog paddle his way through the maze.

Examining the Aric situation was just the sort of labyrinth he was thinking about. Why was the man whapped on the head and left to wander the Village? Why was his wallet taken, his pockets emptied, and then left with what even JB could see was an expensive wristwatch. It did make sense to think that whoever hit Aric probably thought he was dead, and was dumping the body in some New York back alley. But why? Had he seen something he wasn't supposed too? Did he owe money to a loan shark? Was it some sort of revenge thing? There were way to many questions for JB to figure out at this point. And there were only a few ways that he could even think to begin to get any answers.

There was FIT to be looked into. The designer of the coat might be able to supply some information. And Len was going to check on the watch angle too. And Aric was due at Bellevue later that morning. Actual answers would have to start there.

At seven Aric stuck his head through the door and said "Good morning. I took the liberty of making coffee. Would you like some?"

"Sure."

Aric came in and put a cup of black coffee in front of JB. "Do you take it black? It turns out I do."

"This is fine. We have an appointment for you at nine so why don't you go in the bathroom first.

Get ready for your tests."

"What kind of tests do you think they'll do?"

"I would imagine they'll give you an MRI. A brain scan. To see if there's any sustained damage from the hit on the head. If there's any physical cause for the amnesia. After that, who knows?"

Once they had both showered and eaten JB called Len and then waited while he came downstairs from his own apartment to pick up Aric's watch. He was going to take it to a jeweler friend and see if it could be identified.

The watch was a thin round gold faced timepiece with black hands and dashes for numerals. A small square window on the face held an automatic calendar. It had a heavy gold expansion style band, the type that went out of fashion in the sixties. It was the kind of watch worn by power businessmen or Wall Street types back in the day.

"How did you manage to keep this?" JB asked, remembering his earlier thinking.

Aric shook his head. "When I first came to I could feel it tight on my arm. It was shoved way up by my elbow. And under my coat sleeve. Maybe I pushed it there. To save it?"

"To hide it from whoever was attacking you? Could be." One answer down, a million to go. "Anyway, it might provide a clue as to who you are."

Aric handed it over to Len. "Be careful with it. It seems to be all I have."

"I will." He slipped it on his wrist, then held it out to admire it. "I can see why you might have tried to save it. It is a beauty. Vintage. Probably nineteen-sixties. It could be worth some money."

The three men went out and headed for the avenue where they hailed a passing cab. JB knew that it was going to be a taxi sort of day. The subways would take too long and be too much hassle to get to all the places he knew he'd be visiting.

He told the driver to head for Bellevue first, dropping off Len on the way.

"This is a Patek Philippe Swiss watch. This is top of the line, Len. Where did you get it?"

His friend at the jewelry shop had a loupe up to his eye and was examining the watch's back. "It isn't new though." He picked up one of his instruments and pried off the cover. "These watches all have codes engraved on the inside. Two numbers and two letters give the month and year of manufacture. Let's see, this watch was made in June of Nineteen-sixty-five. That makes it worth today around six to eight thousand dollars."

"You're joking? It's worth that much?"

"Would I kid? You might get even ten on a good day at a good auction. What else do you need?"

"I was hoping to find out something about the owner. Can that be traced?"

"You would have to check with the distributor. He could tell you which store handled it. The store might have the information you're looking for. There's another number here. That should be the ID for the American merchandiser."

He wrote down the number and then checked in a loose-leaf binder. "Here it is..." He wrote a name and address on a piece of paper and handed it over to Len. "The distributor is in the diamond district. Around the corner from Radio City. By the way, if you decide to sell that watch, please give me first crack."

Len promised he would and left the shop.

JB had sat with Aric in the Bellevue clinic waiting

area for about forty-five minutes. While they waited JB had made it his business to inform Aric of his patient rights. That the hospital had to have his express permission to do anything with him, and it was up to him to put a stop to any procedure or action that might make him uncomfortable. Even to the point of getting up and leaving the premises if it became necessary.

It wasn't all that unreasonable to think that once Aric was caught up in the mechanics of the Bellevue Hospital system he could disappear. The hospital was famous for their mental facilities so he could easily be thrown into a ward on Bellevue's flight deck and never be heard from again. And JB was savvy enough to know that the police would certainly be among the people interested in his case. That opened a whole other can of creepy crawlies.

When the nurse finally came for Aric, JB told him that when he was finished he should go back to the apartment and handed over an envelope with his address, a set of spare keys, and enough cash for cab fare. The nurse, in an officious way that JB found rather off-putting, said that Aric would probably be spending most of the day at the hospital. There was some real interest in his case among the staff. JB just bet there was. Bellevue was a teaching hospital, so that meant Aric would be seeing multiples of doctors and residents and students throughout the day, along with other staff giving tests, taking blood, and the like. JB assured Aric he would catch up with him no matter what.

He watched his new friend walk off, not really sure he would ever see him again. But there wasn't much choice was there? Aric had to have some medical attention, and the hospital was the best place for that to happen. Bellevue had a number one rating among hospitals in the entire country so there was no worry about the care he'd be given. It was the official state and city bureaucracy that was the worry. They could tie Aric up in knots that even Gordius the king of Phrygia would have wondered at.

JB reluctantly left the hospital and caught another cab.

Len found the distributors offices in the jewelry district and went up the stairs to the offices over the store proper.

Greeted by a wizened bearded little man with Talus fringes hanging below his black suit coat, and the curls of a follower of the Orthodox faith at his ears, Len broached the subject of his inquiry by handing over the timepiece.

"Ah, a good clock. You want to sell, maybe?" The man looked up expectantly.

"Actually I only need to know which store sold the watch originally. Back in sixty-five."

"I think I can do that. We write down the serial numbers in a book." He held up the watch. "You won't mind I open the back?" He pried it open and using a small magnifying glass read off the number. "I have to go to the back. You'll wait?"

It took some kvetching and some coughing and waving at the disturbed dust but finally the man came back to the counter with a leather bound record book marked with the year on the spine. He opened it and wetting a finger he ran it down a column of numbers, finally stopping midway on the page.

"Oy, such an address. Very posh. This watch was consigned to Fulgari. You should be so rich?"

Fulgari's was an up-scale very exclusive jewelers located near Tiffany's on Fifth Avenue. In fact, they considered Tiffany's merely a crass commercial enterprise far beneath their customers social level. One needed an appointment even to look at the merchandise.

Len asked if he could use the phone and called the store's telephone number. After using what cachet his celebrity and his current job on Broadway gave him they agreed to let him in the store a half hour later.

JB got out on the Westside at Twenty-seventh Street and Seventh Avenue in front of FIT—the Fashion Institute of Technology. He had Aric's leather duster hanging over his arm.

He asked a passing kid where he could find admissions and got a grunt along with a raised single finger in reply as the kid continued walking. Heading in the direction the boy's rude bird had indicated, JB entered the steel framed doors on the brick fronted building and found signage that led him to a busy office just inside the main lobby. Behind the front desk was a young woman, probably a student volunteer, sitting under a sign that said *Information.*

JB stood in line while the four people in front of him asked their questions. When he got up to her he asked how he could locate a former student of the school. In a bored perfunctory tone he was directed down a hall and into another office. In there he took a number from a machine on a stand and again waited. Sometimes research was tedious, boring, and annoying. Pulling out the book he had brought with him to read helped some.

A chapter later his number was called and he was led to the desk of a more mature woman than the information girl out front. She also seemed in a far better mood than the younger woman. He asked her if they had a current address for one of their past students. One who went by the name of Aric, with an A. She tapped on a computer keyboard in front of her and waited.

"We have one past student by that name."

"I have no doubt. Not the most common of monikers, right?"

She made no comment, simply looking at him over the top of her glasses. She turned back to the screen. "Let's see. Aric Valenquava. Graduated two years ago with honors. Let me check the alumni information." Tap. Tap. "Yes, here it is. Do you need his business address or his home address?"

"Business, I suppose."

"Located on St. Marks Place." She bent to a stack of yellow *Post-it's*. Tore one off and handed it over. "That's the address. Is there anything else?" All rather cut and dry. JB always appreciated this sort of efficency when he found it. It was becoming harder and harder to find with today's rude and ill mannered young people taking over the world. Or was he just getting crotchety in his rapidly approaching middle aged dotage.

JB began to say no, then remembered. "There is one other thing. I need someone to do a sketch for me. A portrait. Do you know anyone?"

"Not off hand. But check the board in the lobby. Students put up flyers there of their availability. You'll probably find a name there." She turned back to her keyboard and began typing.

"Perfect. Thank you."

Fulgari's was one of those dark marble fronted stores with a dark glass door and a single window beside it. The window was a fourteen by fourteen square lit and recessed into the stone. It was framing an exquisite emerald and diamond necklace which a calligraphed card below it explained once belonged to Queen Alexandria of Russia.

Len pressed the polished brass plated buzzer and waited. Soon enough a man seemingly dressed for a state funeral in a grey ascot and tails opened the door. He looked Len up and down and sneered, "Yes?"

Admittedly Len didn't look upper echelon rich but the attitude really wasn't called for. Just because he was dressed in casual *Dockers*, loafers, and a top coat didn't mean he should be treated like trade. The coat was camel hair after all. He put on his best crusty British accent, "Yes, I called earler. To speak with Mr... What was his name? Oh, pish posh, the manager, my good fellow." He swept past the undertaker into the store.

"Good day." Another gentleman dressed in a dark pinstripe with a club tie spoke from behind a glass case filled with sparkly bibelots. "How may I direct you?"

"To someone who can tell me who purchased this item."

Len pushed up his sleeve exposing the watch. The gentleman looked ever so slightly down and then almost fell over himself as he grinned at Len and asked him to follow. The man literally backed his way to the rear wall and pressed the button for the elevator. "Our Ms. Klank should be able to assist you, sir. On the second floor."

Len nodded, stepped into the now opened doors of the elevator, and looking at his wrist again, vowed that he was going to get one of these watches for himself. Amazing how a little pricey flash could change an attitude.

Ms. Klank turned out to be a zaftig bleached blond with a sweet smile. He showed her the watch and handed over the note with the registration number on it. "Could you check that number and find out who was the original buyer for this item? It's really quite important." He smiled his best eight by ten glossy smile.

"Oh, Mr. Matthews. This is so terrific. You being here. I saw your show just a few weeks ago. It was marvelous. I had such a good time. And you were so good...."

"Thank you. So kind. The watch? Original owner?"

"Oh, of course." She looked at the note. "This is old. It wouldn't be on the computer yet. I'll have to check in the paper files." She stood. "I'll be just a minute. Have a seat." She indicated a gray covered sofa and wiggled off.

He sat and flipped through one of the magazines from the coffee table in front of him. It was an auction catalog of antique jewelry sold at Christies several months earlier. The necklace from the front window was pictured on the front, and estimated to sell for thirty to forty thousand dollars. That meant the store was expecting to get somewhere in the ninety to one-hundred thousand range for the piece in the window.

Ms. Klank came back about fifteen minutes later with a file folder in her hands. She swiped at her skirt and then opened the folder while she sat at her desk. "Dusty back there. Let me see, the information you need should be in here." She turned a few of the pink flimsy pages. "Yes. Here it is. The watch was purchased in September of Sixty-five by the American Ambassador to the UN. Or rather it was his office that bought it. As a gift. We even did the engraving. Two initials in English script. A J and a B. The watch was delivered to their office's at the United Nations building. Does that help?"

"Do you have the name of the person who signed for it?"

"Of course."

This time the cab took JB back to the Eastside and left him off at Avenue A and St. Marks Place. Located in the East Village its main feature was an ever passing parade of the more avent garde of the city's citizens.

Populated with boutiques, art galleries and head shops the street had the most forward, kooky, out there clothes and things anyone could hope for. Brit Punk. Fantasy. Psychedelic. Hippie. Vintage. Clothes and accessory shops were lined all along the way. The lamp posts were even a part of the design, having their bases done in mosaics with pieces of broken china. This was where a young unknown designer or artist could make a name for himself. Aric's shop was on the first floor of an old brownstone over looking the main drag.

JB climbed the stoop and went inside. When he stepped in he was almost overwhelmed by the smell of the leather materials and dyes the designer worked with. Industrial piping racks and tables of metal mesh were stacked and hung with leather goods—purses, coats, pants, skirts. Aric was a prolific designer who was selling his work to a special clientele. At prices that certainly reflected the couture style he brought to the enterprise.

The duster with decorative stitching JB was carrying came in at a cool seven hundred and eighty bucks, at least according to the hang tag on a similar coat draped on a mannequin standing in the center of the shop.

Aric, the designer and sales person, and probably everything else from what JB could see, came out from the back workroom to meet him. He was a young Hispanic man with a goatee, long hair pulled back into a thin ponytail, and heavy lidded dark eyes. Well worn jeans, a white T, and a leather vest was the costume worn by him and most of the other men walking around in the district. Aric had completed his own look by adding multiple piercings at his nose, lips and ears. The silver almost clanked as he walked. He introduced himself in a soft voice with a distinct Cuban accent.

JB explained his reason for coming to the store and got a response that was disheartening to say the least. There were so many of that particular style coat sold that it would be impossible to know who had purchased it. Although the stitching on the one JB had put it at the first season for the design. JB was thanking the designer for his time when he posed his own question. Had JB checked the hidden pocket?

"Hidden?"

"Here in the collar. Turn it up and there is a pocket sewn inside." Aric turned the leather and showed him. JB reached inside and felt something. Pulling out the contents he found a business card and a fifty dollar bill. Emergency money obviously. The card was for an interior design firm—Sterling and Phan Inc.—located just a few blocks away from the shop. Had his Aric been shopping in his own neighborhood? Supporting local business?

JB thanked the young man and started walking to the address on the card.

The flags of the member nations flapped in the breeze as Len walked up the curved drive to the entrance of the fifties mid-century modern building housing the United Nations. Glass and concrete in the curved multi-windowed facade of the General Assembly building. Inside he was directed to the offices of the American delegation. Up the escalator and he was at the elevator bank in the thirty-nine story marble and glass Secretariat building. Then an elevator car took him up to the correct floor. A carpeted hallway directed him to the right office.

Once there he found himself facing an older woman. Late fifties, but very nicely put together. Well made Anne Kline suit, chained half glasses perched on a still pert nose. Lively eyes that would brook no folderol.

"May I help you, sir."

"I hope so." Len again pulled up his coat sleeve. "I have been told that this office purchased this watch back in the Nineteen-sixties. Would it be possible to find out the reason for that?"

She pushed her glasses up and peered at the watch. "My goodness. Believe it or not, I can help you. I remember that watch. It was a retirement gift from the then serving ambassador to one of our people who was leaving. It was my first year here in the office. I had just been hired for the steno pool. We all chipped in for the gift and the ambassador made up the difference. It was quite expensive if I recall."

"And the name of the recipient?"

"Oh, it was for Jack. Jack Bonanno. He'd been with the ambassador for several years, even when the ambassador had been stationed in Canada. He was leaving us to open his own hotel. A bed and breakfast in an old Victorian he'd bought. Now where was that? My goodness, the memory isn't what it once was." Her face screwed up trying to remember, then relaxed when she had it. "Oh yes, it was in Yonkers."

Yonkers? That was the second time in as many days he'd heard of that city. Strange. Bet JB would be interested in that. "You've been so helpful. Would it be possible to check the records and find an address for Mr. Bonanno?"

"That would be in the HR office. It's down the hall. I'll call and tell them you're coming."

The studio of Sterling and Phan was a storefront turned to an office with a large open cut neon sign on the top flashing the name of a previous tenant. A dry cleaners. The front window had the name of the interior design firm painted in black and outlined with gold. Behind that was a set of white Venetian blinds closed to the afternoon sun.

JB opened the door and stepped into a retro fifties living room with Chinese modern accessories. There were painted screens and flower filled urns scattered about. A Frank Lloyd Wright Prairie style desk was set by the door. Behind it was a young man of about twenty. Or sixteen. At any rate very young looking. He was the type that would be stunning when he finally matured, now he just looked sort of pimply. Dressed in a two colored diamond patterned knitted cardigan sweater and slacks he fit right in with the vibe of the studio. He smiled—he had good straight teeth—and stood. "How may I help you?" He sounded even younger than he looked, as if his voice hadn't quite made the change to adulthood.

JB introduced himself and asked if he was the owner.

"Oh dear, no. I'm only the intern. I help around here. Answering phones, making coffee, making appointments for Mr. Phan and Mr. Sterling. They're very busy people." There was a bit of snobbery in his answer. Expected from Upper Eastsiders maybe, but borderline rude here in the Village.

"Then they're who I would want to talk to. Are they here?"

"Unfortunately, no. Mr. Phan is out on a call. Servicing a client, as he often is. And Mr. Sterling is out of town. Maybe I can put you down in the book for a better time?"

JB noticed a clear plastic holder with several brochures standing upright in it. He took one and opened it. Advertising the firm's decorating and antique acquisition services, it also featured a picture of the two owner's standing side by side with what they hoped were winning smiles on their faces. Mr. Phan was an Asian man who looked to be somewhere in his twenties. Although he could have also been in his teens. He looked young. He was pretty rather than handsome. Slight, with black longish hair that gave him even more of an effeminate air. The other man, identified as Mr. Sterling, was most certainly his Aric. Peter Sterling and the amnesiac known as Aric were one and the same person. Aric had thought he had maybe been an architect—interior design was a close enough relative.

"You said Mr. Sterling was out of town?"

"That's right. He had to attend a conference upstate. But he's due back tomorrow. Would you like an appointment for then?"

"And Mr. Phan?"

"His partner. He had a consultation with a client today. He'll also be here tomorrow. Should I put you down for noon?"

"Sure. Put down J. Bent. But make it for eleven. Tomorrow."

"J. Bent. The writer?"

"That's right."

"Then I'll make sure to tell Mr. Phan."

"If it will get me better service feel free?

CHAPTER 6

W hen the last cab of the day dropped JB off at his apartment he walked into his building lobby and found that his front door was unlocked and open a few inches. A sick feeling shot through him—someone had invaded his space, an intruder had violated his home.

He pushed the door and saw Aric—except

now JB had to think of him as Peter—sitting on his couch in what could only be called an agitated state. Relief flooded through JB. His home was still safe after all.

When Peter saw him he stood. "My God, I'm so glad you're here, JB. I've been sitting for an hour thinking the cops were going to burst through the door."

"They wouldn't have to when you leave the door open." He shut the door and shot the lock to closed. "What happened."

"Well, I stood still for the tests. And at least twenty or more doctors looking and prodding at me. They did do a brain scan like you said they would."

"Did they tell you the results?"

"The main doctor said that I did have a mild concussion but there's no permanent damage. He thinks this amnesia thing is most likely psychological. So he referred me to a psychiatrist."

Not a surprise, JB was thinking. Bellvue is a psychiatric hospital. A shrink would be their go to person for most any ailment.

"I met with him for an hour or so," Peter went on. "But then the police stepped in. They took me to this office where they fingerprinted me. Then they left me alone. For a long time. So I took your advice. You know when you said if I was uncomfortable I should leave. That's what I did. I got scared, JB. I knew they were going to keep me there. So I got up and I left. But they know where I'm staying. Your address. They'll come after me."

"You said its been an hour?" He nodded. "Then they probably don't think you're any great threat. If they did they probably would have beat you here." JB went to the bathroom and got another two Valium for Peter. "Here take these. Then I'll fill you in on what I found out."

Still shaking he took the pills as JB asked.

JB sat beside Peter on the couch. "Does the name Peter Sterling mean anything to you?"

He thought for a moment. "It seems familiar, but I don't know why."

"How about Phan? Does that elicit anything? That's P-H-A-N."

"That's odd. It does. It sent a tingle through me. Why is that?"

"It means the Swiss cheese that your memory currently is connects the name with something. Probably something good considering the tingle. Here. Take a look at this." JB handed over the brochure he had taken from the interior design firm. "Your real name seems to be Peter Sterling. Your business partner—or more likely he's something more—is named Phan. That's pretty good proof of who you are."

Peter stared at the picture of the two of them. "That is me, all right. But I have no idea who this other one is. Is it this Phan person?" JB nodded. "Then I should know him, shouldn't I? But I don't. Crap." He threw the brochure on the coffee table. "This is awful. This not knowing. This bits and pieces existence I'm having." He started to cry but wiped at the tears angrily.

"Come on, Peter. This will work itself out. Already you're having partial memories. As we find out more the rest will surely fall in place. I know it. Listen, I made us an appointment to meet with this Phan person tomorrow. That will go a long way to making you feel better."

The buzzer rang. Someone was outside. Peter went immediantly back into panic mode. "They're here. The cops. They've come for me..."

"You don't know that. Wait just a second." JB went to the intercom and said, "Hello, who is it?"

A tinny voice came back. "It's Jerome. Jerome Marsh. From FIT. You called me to work for you."

JB pushed the button that let him into the lobby, then turned to Peter. "It's the artist I hired to come and do a sketch for me. So relax, it isn't the police." There was a knock on the door. "If you're still uncomfortable why don't you go to the kitchen and make us some coffee. It will help calm you down, and keep you busy while I talk with this guy."

Peter did exactly that while JB opened the door. The young man standing at the door had a sketch pad under his arm and a briefcase in one hand. "Come in. The person I wanted you to talk with isn't here right now, but he should be here soon. What I'm asking for is the sort of thing that the police do on *Cagney and Lacey*. Make a likeness from a description of somebody. You can do that?"

"Oh, sure. I've done courtroom sketches before. And portraits also."

"Sounds good. Would you like some coffee while we wait?"

The young man sat while JB went to the kitchen. He was back in less than a minute with a tray Peter had put together. Cups, coffee, cream, sugar, and a dish of store bought *Entenman's* mint chocolate chip cookies. JB set it in front of Jerome and said, "Help yourself."

He looked at his watch. "Now. where the hell is Len? He should have his mobil phone with him. I'll try that number." JB dialed his old fashioned black rotary phone. It was a relic, true, picked up at an antique store in the same vicinity as The Strand Bookstore, and was a reminder from his childhood. Sometimes JB felt technology didn't really need to replace everything. Some things worked just fine without adding fancy lights and ringing bells. Once connected he found out Len was in a cab just pulling up to East Sixty-fourth Street.

Len was then knocking on the door almost before

JB hung up the phone.

"JB, I swear, you have got to stop these Inspector Clouseau quests you keep sending people on. I have been all over the island of Manhattan today. My feet are an absolute nub." He hung his coat on the rack by the door and flopped onto the unoccupied chair. "And who are you?" he said, noticing Jerome, who had done a little spit take with his coffee when he saw Len Matthews walk into the room.

"That, Len, is the artist who is going to make a sketch of your AA assassin. Jerome, meet Len Matthews. He'll describe the person for your drawing."

He gushed. "A pleasure, Mr. Matthews. I loved you in *The Odd Couple.*"

"Really? Thank you, but that was Tony Randall."

"Oh. Sorry. You can't win em' all."

"You haven't won any yet."

Jerome slunk into the couch. Len spoke to JB.

"And when am I supposed to do this interview with Pablo Picasso here? Unlike some of us, I'm a working man. I have a show tonight." He checked his watch. "I'm due at the theater in an hour."

"You could take Jerome with you. Do it there. He is, I'm sure, a movable artist."

Jerome nodded, happy at the thought of getting to go backstage at a Broadway theater.

Peter, standing at the kitchen door, said. "Isn't that watch mine?"

"You are correct, sir." Len said, doing an Ed MacMahon with Karnac the Magician impression. He removed the clock from his wrist. "But I'm getting one of these for myself. You have no idea how doors open when its visible." He held the watch over his head. "I may have one attached as a tiara." Then he lowered it. "Or a nose ring." He held it out to Peter.

Peter took the watch and slipped it back on his own wrist. He clasped his hand over it, as if to protect it, or to make himself feel comforted. "Then you found out something about it? Is it worth money?" he asked.

"Several thousand dollars, if you must know."

"No shit?" He sat on the couch staring at the timepiece.

"What else did you find, Len? Did you find the original owner?" JB sat across from him.

"Well, yes and no. I found out who it was."

"That's the yes?"

"But I'm afraid he's no longer living."

"And that's the no?"

"Does the name Jack Bonanno mean anything to you?" Len looked at Peter.

He went pale. His face contorted as he fought to keep in control. Tears misted his eyes, then began to leak onto his cheek. Then he gave up, completely broke and began to sob into his hands.

"I'm going to guess the name has some meaning for you?"

Peter nodded. "That's Papa. Jack Bonanno was my father."

JB turned to him. "Wait. We just found out your name is Peter Sterling. It isn't then?"

Len looked confused, as did Jerome. JB showed them the brochure and explained what he had found out during the day.

"Then he's two people. How can that be?"

"If I knew would I be scratching my head?"

"That could be a bad case of dandruff."

"No, its too many questions causing my head to ache. What else did you find on this Bonanno person?"

"Okay, he worked at the UN as an aide to the US ambassador up until Nineteen-sixty-five. Then he left to open a hotel."

Peter said, "And both he and his wife, my mother, were killed in a car crash. I was seventeen."

"So, Nineteen-sixty-nine."

Peter went on, memories flooding, doors slipping open a crack. "I was drafted at eighteen. Sent to Nam. Stationed in Saigon. Attached to the embassy there. Evacuated in Seventy-three. Before the fall though. I came back home early. Oh, my God, I was wounded." He felt his right leg. "Here. That's why I came home. With a medical discharge."

"Where was home, Peter?"

"I think...No, I don't know where."

Len answered. "Yonkers. You lived in Yonkers. That's where your father's hotel was. And ain't that a kick, JB? I found that article about Yonkers just yesterday."

JB was indeed surprised. The town of Yonkers coming up twice in as many days? Coincidence could be a bitch. "Len, we need that sketch of your guy from the AA rooms. He might somehow be connected to Peter."

"That's a reach, JB, exceeding even your well honed imagination." Len sighed. "And you're going up there, aren't you? To Yonkers? I should have known. Here you go jumping of the cliff again."

"It's intriguing, Len. You have to admit that, don't you?"

"What I have to do is get to work." Len pointed at Jerome. "Come on, Renoir, you come with me"

Jerome stood. "I'll do the sketch and leave it with Mr. Matthews. Uh, at the agreed on price."

"Of course." JB pulled out his wallet and handed over a fifty dollar bill."

"Well, come on, Chagall. Let's go." Len was getting into his coat. Jerome picked up his things and the two men left.

JB turned back to Peter who was slouched on the couch deep in confused thought. "I don't understand, JB."

"You can't be expected to. It's just become more confused for all of us, Peter. We're going to have to go up to Yonkers tomorrow. We can go after our meeting with Mr. Phan at his design studio. Its going to be a full day."

CHAPTER 7

Peter and JB were on time for their appointment at the interior design firm. They stepped up to the front door at exactly eleven o'clock. It was locked so JB pushed the button and heard a bell ring inside.

Several moments later the door was opened by the other person pictured in the brochure JB had picked up the day before. Mr. Phan looked in life as he was pictured in print. Pretty and quite effeminate. His manner was also very graceful, and a couple of shades to far this side of nellie for JB's taste. All swinging hips and sweeping gestures he asked them inside. He had a silky voice shaded by a lisp, along with a soup-con of a foreign accent. Not Japanese, but Asian for sure. A hint of vaguely French pronunciation on certain words led JB to think him most likely Vietnamese. Part of the wave of refugee's that had come to the US after the end of the war fourteen or so years before.

"I wonder where you had got off to, Peter," he said. He was wearing a Japanese patterned silk kimono with the long sleeves that the fashion demanded. As he spoke his waving arms caused the sleeves to swing wildly. Almost pouting he went on. "When did you get back? And why didn't you come home straight?" He then looked at JB. "And who is this one you picked up? Another of your tricks?"

"I...I. No, you don't understand...."

He didn't give Peter a chance to go on. "I understand plenty. The Carlsons called. They wonder what had happened since you didn't make appointment with them. Is this what held you up?" He pointed a manicured finger at JB, making him think of Madam Ginsling from those thirties movies featuring Anna May Wong. JB could tell he was angry, it oozed throughout his voice, but he didn't actually look it. His face remained placid, even calm, although JB wouldn't have been the least surprised if a Chinese throwing star wasn't lobbed into his chest in the next few moments.

JB stepped forward into the fray. "Really, Mr. Phan. You're making a huge mistake. Please let me explain..." JB went on to tell Phan what had happened to Peter and the reason behind his missing the appointment he had mentioned.

Phan's manner then changed completely. Sugar replaced the sour. He stepped forward, leaned against Peter and cooed, "Oh, Peter, I am sorry. I had no idea."

For his part, Peter simply stood there. He didn't recoil, but he did stiffen. He was clearly uncomfortable.

Phan looked up at him, his face contorted, a mood change swung into place, and he stepped back. "You don't know me? Is that it?", he shrilled. "It is years we have been together, and you don't know me?" He wouldn't have been out of place in a Kabuki drama as he said this. His expression exaggerated beyond exaggeration, all gnashing teeth and upraised eyebrows. JB was thinking he just might begin tearing out clumps of his hair. A real drama queen this one.

Peter simply looked pained. "I'm sorry, but I don't. I hoped I would, but no." He shook his head. "Oddly enough, I do know some things about you. Like you take your coffee with three sugars. Intimate things too. You sit to pee. You're passive in bed. I know that. I must remember that. So there has to be some connection. But I don't know what it is,"

Phan turned away, his arm covering his face. It was overly dramatic gesture 101 from Madam Butterfly U. A moment and then he turned back. His performance wasn't over. He was showing every effort to keep himself in check. To keep himself from screaming at what he must have seen as some breach of faith on Peter's part. A silent screen actress couldn't have played the scene better. Then he stood straight. His face went hard. "Come with me," he said tightly. He turned and sashayed to the rear of the office.

Peter looked over at JB, who shrugged back. They followed him. When Phan got to a set of metal industrial stairs he stopped.

"You and me live above" He started up the stairs. "Come up. We talk there."

They followed him up.

The apartment was a living room and a galley kitchen decorated in the same Asian Modern style as the office downstairs. There were low couches, silk painted hangings, bonsai trees, and laquered folding screens everywhere. It reminded JB of the sort of place Hollywood would have us believe a Chinese whorehouse looks like. A bedroom and a bathroom was off the rear. At the front was a set of sliding glass doors that looked out on the roof of the office below, which had been worked into a stone and gravel patio with a container garden and lounge area built onto the asphalt. A gold painted Buddha beatifically stared back at them. The back of the cutout neon sign for the dry cleaning business was shadowed in the morning sun, blocking the roof from the view of people down on the street.

"Sit, please. Now, what can we do to make this better?"

"Perhaps if you start by telling Peter some of your history, Phan. His memory is in pieces. Something you say might trigger a recollection."

"All right. I am Phan Tok. I come to the US with my parent in Nineteen-seventy-five after the fall of Saigon. I was thirteen. Peter and I met seven years ago. In Nineteen-eighty."

So Phan was twenty-five. Older than JB had guessed. And a ten year difference between him and Peter. "Where was that?"

"Here. New York City. I love the US. And your westerns especially. We meet at the Lone Star Cafe. At concert of Kinky Friedman. You remember? I am crazy for country music."

"So is Peter." That explained his recognition of Reba McEntire's new single wafting from a bar on

Christopher Street.

Phan nodded, then went on. "We open this business five years ago. Peter has background as architect and I went to Parsons for interior and furniture design. We have done well. Does any of this help?" He looked at Peter.

Peter looked around the apartment. "All of this seems familiar to me. But that's it. It isn't like I know this is where I belong." He hesitated a moment, then spoke to Phan. "Then you and I are lovers? Is that right? I'm gay then?"

"Of course."

"Then why don't I feel comfortable? Can you explain that to me? JB, if I'm gay I should have some sort of tender feelings for him, right? But I don't. I'm sorry, Phan, I don't. I don't feel like I even know you." Peter was becoming more agitated. "I'm sorry. None of this rings any bells. I don't remember this. And I don't remember what our relationship was."

JB put his hand on Peter's shoulder. "It's okay. It will just take time."

"Bull. That's all I've been hearing for two days now. From you. From the doctors. And my life isn't coming back. This is ridiculous. Why can't I remember?"

"Hey, we only found out last night that your real name is Peter. Give it some time."

Phan stood from his chair. "He is correct. Why don't we have lunch. The three of us. Then I tell you more about our lives together."

Peter said, "No. We can't. We have some place else we have to go. Don't we, JB."

"But I have albums, Peter. Pictures of us. Together. From last summer at Fire Island. And the trip to Nantucket. It might bring back memories. And this is your home. You should stay."

"Actually, Peter, you don't have to go with me.

And what I have to do might not even concern you. It's more Len's thing. I think lunch is a good idea. It will give Phan here a chance to tell you more about yourself. Any one piece of information might be the one thing that brings it all back. Why don't you stay and look at the albums?"

Peter argued that he didn't want to impose, but Phan said it wouldn't be a bother. Then Peter said he wasn't hungry, but Phan offered to make a light snack instead of something heavier. His objections being all washed away Peter finally agreed to stay.

JB begged off from having lunch, saying he did indeed have another place he had to go to. He gathered his things and both Phan and Peter walked him down the stairs and to the front door. Phan held out his hand limply while JB gingerly shook it, almost afraid it might shatter if gripped to hard. Then he turned to Peter, who grabbed him and pulled him close. He hugged him until JB said, "Hey, honey, you're going to turn me into a diamond if you don't loosen up."

Peter quickly let go and stood back. "Sorry, JB. I'm just so thankful for your help."

"Sure." JB looked him in the eye. "Call me if you need me. Okay."

He left Peter and Phan to try and put their lives back into one piece.

JB was sort of hoping that when he arrived at the Yonkers Station on the Metro North he would find a setting out of *Hello Dolly*. Gingerbread trimmed roofs, horse drawn carriages. A Currier and Ives landscape. Instead what he found was more out of present day Brooklyn or Queens.

It had been a leisurely and quiet trip out from the city. The train had rolled past the backs of detached two story duplexes and brick industrial buildings almost close enough to touch. Streets with small children running and playing peeked between. It had only taken about fifteen minutes to ride up from Penn Station since Yonkers was only a couple of miles away from Manhattan. But George M. Cohan had it right when his song said it was totally different. A fine bunch of rubens indeed. Yonkers was far more suburban than urban. It was also way more bigoted than JB was comfortable with, since the city schools hadn't even integrated yet—despite the laws. He affected a Robert Mitchum macho walk as he left the station in case there were bands of villagers with torches waiting outside.

He headed toward the Chamber of Commerce building on Main Street thinking he might be able to get the information he was looking for there. Was there a B&B once owned by a Jack Bonanno in town, and was it still open? Maybe being run by a relative who could explain how Peter Sterling was the son of said Jack. He also meant to look into the death of the woman who might be connected to Len's newly sober assassin. That he would check out at the newspaper offices of the *Yonkers Star.*

JB climbed the stairs to the second floor and the Chamber's offices. Inside he first looked at a rack holding leaflets about the wonders of Yonkers— Sarah Lawrence College, the old Otis Elevator Company building (turned the year before into the Kawasaki railroad assembly plant, where the new cars for New York's subways came from), and the views of the Hudson River from the Palisades. Pictured were a row of several Victorian mansions that overlooked the area.

JB carried the folder to the woman behind the desk and used it to illustrate what he was asking. If there was a Jack Bonanno who once owned any of these homes in the area. Len had said that the

UN secretary lady had mentioned that it was an old Victorian that the man had purchased.

The woman immediately said no, then stopped. "Wait, let me ask Mary. She's been here much longer than I have. She might know better." JB waited while she went off to find the other woman.

Mary was an older woman, near or past retirement at any rate, and looked it. Grey hair in a knot on top of her head and a roadmap of wrinkles on her face. "Now what is it your asking, young man?" Her voice quivered, as if doing a Katherine Hepburn impression. "Jack Bonanno, was it? He died years ago. In a car accident."

"So you did know him? Good. What I wondered was if he owned a hotel here. And if he had a son? Did he?"

"He did run a hotel. Turned the old Taylor mansion into a bed and breakfast. Over on Hudson Terrace. In the Northwest section of town. Beautiful place. And he fixed it up real nice. But he died, like I said. A year or so after he opened the place."

"And what happened to it after that? Were there any heirs?"

"I assume his boy inherited. Whoever it was kept the place running for years and years. Right up until, let's see, Nineteen-eighty, I guess. That's when Miss Stymington closed it and just lived in the house."

"Then Miss Stymington is the current owner."

"That's right."

"Could you give me the address of the house. Do you know it?"

"Of course I do. I'm old not senile, young man."

She was back with the address in moments. JB thanked her and then left the office. Once more on the street he had to decide what was next. He wanted to look into the accident that had killed Mr. Bonanno. And find out who was the boy that was left behind. He also wanted to check out the house that he now had an address for. And he wanted to see what the newspapers might not have mentioned in the article about the woman that was killed the other day. So it was either the library or the newspaper office. Which was closest? He had no idea. A moment later he went back upstairs for directions.

Turned out it was the newspaper office, only a few blocks away on Central Avenue. JB followed the directions he had been given and ended up at Central Park Avenue according to the signage. Was it the same? He spotted the *Yonkers Star* placard on a building down the street. Must be. It's probably the same thing that New Yorkers do—refusing to call The Avenue Of The Americas anything other than Sixth Avenue, despite its name being changed decades before.

The newspaper offices were housed in a brick fronted building with the name of the paper in one-hundred and eighty point pica type and gold leafed lettering arched on the front window. JB stepped up to the counter and waited. A young girl, around seventeen or so, came from the back. "Can I help you?" A pretty girl, hair in a feathered Farrah Fawcett cut, wearing jeans and a sweater with football player sized shoulder pads, she smiled pleasantly.

"Yes please. I was wondering if I could get some information about a residence here in Yonkers.?

"A house? Which one?"

"It used to be the Taylor place. Then it was a B&B. Now its a private residence."

"Oh, you mean an old place." Anything before Nineteen-seventy was probably old to her. "Let me get Tony. He's the town historian around here."

Tony was about thirty, handsome, with brown hair, dark blue eyes, and a very cute butt. Full name: Tony Kilbreth. This could turn out to be more interesting that first thought. JB felt a tiny stirring in his nether regions. It had been a couple of months since he'd been properly laid and quiescent urges were waking from their slumber. Attractive men could do that to him.

"Hi." He held out his hand. "My name is Jeremy Bent. JB for short. I'm a writer here from the city, and I'm doing some research on the local area. Specifically a Victorian that was turned into a B&B in the late sixties." When Tony took his hand JB felt a tingle go through him. Lust was definitely on the rise.

Tony smiled a most charming smile. Tingles intensified. "Several of our older houses here in town have gone commercial over the years. We have back issues of the paper on micro-fiche back that far. You're welcome to look through them."

"That would be great."

Tony led JB back—with JB leering most appreciatively at his ass as they did—to a large library table that held the machine and a rack of the cassettes that worked with it. It was a great hooded black metal affair with a large glass screen inside for projecting the photographic content on the cassettes. There were two small silver wheels on each side which would run the pages forward or backward. Tony flipped a switch and it clicked on, lit up, and emitted a low hum. JB sat down on a wooden backed chair in front of the behemoth and looked into the hooded screen area.

"What year was it you said?" Okay, now even his voice was causing JB to stir. The timber of it, the low growl it purred, sent endorphins running along nerve ends throughout his body.

"Uh, Nineteen-sixty-five was the year the hotel opened."

Tony checked the rack, pulled out the proper

cassette, marked with the year on its side, and stuck it into the slot. The mechanics were all on the same order as a VCR, but the technology had been around much longer. The machine's screen projected an image of the first page of *The Yonkers Star* from January of the year requested.

"The paper was a bi-weekly back then. So there are twenty-six issues a year. Now we run every three days. Mostly it's a shopping paper now, but we slip in local news where we can."

"Thanks. This will help a lot."

He leaned over JB's shoulder. JB cringed at the odor rising off him. "You know how to work one of these?" he asked. Tony smelled of aftershave and print paper, a combination sure to win JB's writers heart.

"From years ago. New York mostly uses computers now."

"We've been talking about going to computers here. Haven't quite made the decision yet. Well, I'll leave you to your project." JB was ready to cry. He wanted to leap up and bodily tackle the man. "Would you like something to drink? We have a soda machine"

"That would be great."

He sauntered off, leaving JB feeling suddenly lost, alone and horny. Damn, why was it that he was so easily led around by his dick. The thing had a mind entirely it's own, and would pop up, so to speak, at the most inopportune times. There was business to be done, and the more monkey type business his brain was presently contemplating was not on the agenda. He slapped his overactive gonads back into line and focused on his research.

Even back in the sixties the newspaper relied heavily on advertising so he scanned quickly looking for ads that referred to the B&B. He found the first in the month of June. Advertising the grand opening of Hudson River House, newly furbished and owned by Jack and Sara Bonanno. It was a half page ad with a B&W picture of the house itself. Situated up a short flight of stairs it was a bit reminiscent of the *Psycho* house from the Hitchcock movie, but in much better condition. Even in the old picture the place looked newly painted and spic and span clean.

A few days later the paper ran a full article about the B&B. It introduced Jack and Sara, and talked about their ambitions for the hotel. Then, in passing, mentioned their only son, Nicholas, who was then thirteen. That's the right age for Peter. Could it be Peter? Then what's the name change about?

Peter had said his parents died in a car accident when he was seventeen. That would have been Nineteen-sixty-nine. JB ran his finger over the cassettes, found the right year, and slid it into the machine.

The accident was front page news. Slippery roads after a night of drinking at the local nightclub had the couple skidding to their deaths. Instantaneously. Further searching of the articles found that the hotel was taken over by Jack's brother, Sam, and his wife, after the funeral. There was no mention of Nicholas, except as a survivor.

No mention until a few months later when it relayed that he had gone into the service and was expected to be shipped to Vietnam in the near future. Drafted was more like it. He'd turned eighteen only weeks after his parents were taken and probably got his notice from the local draft board soon after his graduation from high school. The authorities at that point—that would be Nineteen-seventy—in the unpopular war were desperate for any body they could get. Quotas needed to be filled. So off Nicholas went.

This time the paper printed one of those bootcamp pictures of the newly appointed soldier. Looking shone like a sheep and with abject fear in his eyes, the eighteen year old boy pictured might have been Peter, or he could have been Gore Vidal, or Truman Capote for that matter. It was difficult, if not impossible, to add seventeen years onto the grainy pixilated picture the paper had used.

The lady at the Chamber of Commerce had said the hotel was open until Nineteen-eighty. That's a long time for a business to keep going. Most business closed in the first five years. Why had it been shut down after fifteen?

JB pulled out the cassette for Nineteen-eighty. Sure enough the hotel had been closed that year. Due to unforeseen circumstances it said. What were they?

JB skimmed the pages back and forth around the announcement of the closing. Then he found an article that explained it.

Nicholas Bonanno, then proprietor of Hudson River House, had disappered. He had gone out on a fishing trip to the river one morning and been lost. His boat was found, empty, and he was presumed drowned, although there was no body ever found. His wife, Rosalie, had decided to close the hotel since she felt it more than she could handle on her own. So Nicholas had married had he? And then drowned. Did he?

Peter had said he came back from Vietnam in Nineteen-seventy-three as a wounded vet. Giving him recovery time he might have returned to Yonkers in early seventy-four. JB reached for that years cassette.

There it was. April seventy-four. Nicholas Bonanno married his high school sweetheart. One Rosalie Stymington. Daughter of a wealthy judge in the Yonkers municipal court system. Stymington? Why was that name familiar? Of course, the Chamber woman had said she was the current owner of the house. She still lived in Hudson River House, even after her husband disappeared? But there was something else. The name rang some other bells. Why? At any rate, JB would definitely have to go see this house for himself.

The wedding occasioned the paper to run a larger and better picture of Nicholas and Rosalie. The groom was twenty-one by then and was looking more grown up. And it was definitely Peter Sterling. Or a damn close approximation. Was there a twin thing? Or something more devious at work?

Tony, the newspaper's historian, came back and asked if JB was finding everything he needed. And the tingles started again. But JB tamped them down again. There was still Len's alcoholic killer he hadn't done anything about. He asked if there was any information on the lady who had been shot a few days eariler.

"That wouldn't be on the micro-fiche yet. I'll get you the hard copies. Wait just a moment."

While he waited JB gathered together the multiple reproductions of the articles he had been reading all afternoon. He checked his watch. Good God, it was already after five. He had lost the whole day putting this old story together. And even now there were a shitload of questions still unanswered.

Tony came back with the papers and laid them down in front of JB. He handed over the top paper. "This is from the day she was shot. The others are mostly a rehash of the facts."

JB looked over the article Tony had pointed out. A name jumped off the page and seared itself like steak grill marks into his conscienceness. Rosalie Stymington was the woman who had been killed! She was the one who had been shot in cold blood on the widows walk of her Victorian mansion only a few days before. On the day before Aric/Peter/ Nicholas, with a fresh head wound, showed up at the Gay Community Center in New York City.

CHAPTER 8

Since it was so late that the entire newspaper had emptied of all the employees except Tony, JB helped him close the office, then took him three doors down the street to the first bar they found for a friendly nightcap.

It turned out to be one of those new sports theme bars. Dedicated to any game that used a ball it reeked of stale testosterone and beer. JB felt like an Atheist at a Catholic picnic. But he had his reasons for buying Tony a drink. He wanted to do a bit of a quizzing of the man. JB had questions and maybe Tony could supply answers. Plus he was still feeling that horndog attraction to him. More might come out of it than answers...

"The woman who was killed," JB asked. "What do you know about the case? As a reporter you'd have access to the cops around here. Do they have any idea who did it?"

Tony took a sip of his beer. "They don't have much. She was shot by a single bullet right to the forehead. But they didn't find any spent casings near the body. Since it was a clean shot they think it was a sniper shooting from a distance. A pretty good one I have to think."

"Okay. Now that seems odd. You have a lot of snipers roaming around Yonkers do you?"

"Miss Stymington was the first person actually murdered in Yonkers in over a year. Other than domestic disputes that is. So the answer would be no. Not a lot of snipers."

"But a sniper would indicate that some unknown person wanted her killed. Unless it was just random. Have there been any others?"

"Not so far. Yonkers isn't Kent State."

"Then why would she be targeted?"

"She was, according to the police, just a nice woman who lived alone and didn't cause anyone any trouble. She didn't seem to be mixed up in anything nefarious or illegal. She lived by herself in that big old house. She was a widow. Her husband drowned several years ago. It's a mystery."

"My bread and butter, by the way."

Tony looked mystified himself.

"Mysteries. I write them. And this is one hell of a one. I need to find out some more about this lady."

"Well, I would talk to her lawyer then. He's got an office here in town. He's probably handling her affairs. The will and all. I'll give you his name." He grabbed a napkin to write on.

"Good idea. You think like I do. Must be the reporter in you." JB smiled his most ingratiating smile. "We could make a good team. You and I. Why don't we work together on this?" And he reached out and patted Tony on the thigh.

"Uh, I don't think I would have the time." He crossed his leg. Which effectively removed it from JB's reach. "The newspaper keeps me pretty busy."

"Oh, all right. Then maybe we could have dinner?" Tony's eyes narrowed. "I have some more questions..."

Tony took a large sip of his beer. "Well, thanks, but I need to get home. The wife is waiting. But thanks for the offer." He finished his beer and stood. "Nice to meet you, Mr. Bent." And he ran out of the bar.

That, JB realized after the fact, had been exceedingly awkward. And downright mortifying. An intercepted pass—called so to fit with the surrounding decor. Not a touchdown, a fumbled forward pass. JB felt like an idiot. What had happened to his gaydar? He wasn't normally wrong about these things, but he sure was this time. Oh, well. Nothing ventured, nothing gained? Nothing gained all right. Except the calories from a now unwanted beer.

JB caught the train back to Manhattan.

Once back in the city he headed off walking toward Broadway, intending to stop at the theatre to see Len. He had checked his phone messages before leaving Yonkers and Len had asked him to stop by his dressing room that evening. Never an arduous task and the walk would do JB some good. Also Len would want to know what JB had learned from his excursion.

Backstage the last hour before curtain is like a warren of busy mice all performing their assigned tasks. Prop people check to make sure everything is lined up according to the script cues. Costume people get wardrobe in place for quick changes between scenes. Sets are reviewed to make sure actors won't find misplaced pieces of furniture. The musicians work their way to the pit and begin tuning up for the overture. In the dressing room halls there is a quiet that falls as actors go inside themselves to prepare for their upcoming performances.

JB stopped at the backstage entrance and checked in with the guard. The days of all doormen being called Pops or Gramps had disappeared with the Ziegfeld Follies. Now you had uniformed union security guards with pistols on their hips.

He went up the stairs to Len's door, the one with a silver star on it, and knocked lightly. His dresser, Bobby, answered, put a finger to his lips, then beckoned him inside. Len was sitting in front of the lighted mirror, in a refurbished Nineteen-forties barber chair, with his eyes closed and deep in meditation. Preparing.

JB tiptoed over to the couch and sat, folded his hands, and waited for Len to come out of his trance. Which he did a minute later.

"Okay, Bobby, let's get this sucker on the boards." Bobby stepped up behind Len and helped him put on the white yak hair wig with mutton chop sideburns he wore as the character of Mr. VanRoddy in the play. Then he went to the door to signal Len's make-up guy to glue the wig's edges down and comb it in place. As he did Len said, "Hey, JB, how was the trip? Did you find out anything?"

"As a matter of fact I did. Are you up for it?"

"I've got fifteen minutes before I go on. Sure. What's up?"

JB handed over the sheaf of copies from *The Yonkers Star.* "Take a look at those. Especially the picture of the wedding couple. Now is that Peter or is that Peter? Or rather Nicholas. Or whoever the hell he is."

"Damn. Mysteriouser and mysteriouser, huh?"

"You have no idea…" JB went on to explain about the meeting with Phan—who was more than just a partner in the interior design business. It turned out he had been Peter's lover for the last seven years. On top of that Peter now looked to also be Nicholas, the missing husband of Rosalie Bonanno nee Stymington, a Yonkers housewife. Who also just happened to be the woman who was killed by a strange man Len heard confess to her murder in the AA rooms only a day or two before. "We have got to find this man from the rooms, Len."

Len pulled a piece of paper from the debris on his table. "Well, here's the sketch Jerome did. Maybe it will help."

JB took the picture and looked at it. "You didn't say he was the spitting image of GI Joe, for craps sake."

"I told you he was handsome. And that is a good likeness of the man, JB. I don't forget pretty men. You know that."

"So we're looking for a Hasbro toy? This isn't just a picture of a fantasy boyfriend is it?"

"Of course not. That's what the man looked like. He was a bit more disheveled maybe. More rough, and with a days growth of beard, but that's him.

Some hunk, huh? Jerome and I cleaned him up some. Made him more presentable."

"You're not taking him to meet your mother, Len. He's a suspect in a killing. And we've got to find him."

"And how are we going to do that, JB? He only gave his first name at the meeting I was at. And he left before the meeting was over. Remember he was newly sober. With only a day or so. You know how fragile newbies are. He could have gone out that same night. He seemed that upset."

"But he did talk about it in a meeting. That might indicate that he really didn't want to drink, right? So he would probably keep going to meetings even if he did have to start over. To get himself sober. Our only choice is to go to as many meetings as possible, with this picture in hand, and ask if anyone has seen him."

"Do you have any idea how many AA meetings there are on any given day in New York City. They must number in the hundreds. There is at least one every hour, if not on the half-hour, right up until midnight. He could go to any one of them."

"We'll have to start where you saw him first. Anyway, it'll do you good. The more meetings you make the soberer you get."

"That's not the way it works, JB. It's not quantity, its quality."

There was a knock on the door. "Ten minutes, Mr. Matthews," the call boy shouted. Len stood. Bobby came at him with a bottle green frockcoat which he slipped onto Len's arms.

"Stay, JB." Len bent to check his makeup and hair in the mirror. "We'll talk more at intermission."

"I was thinking, while Betty was doing her

monologue—I swear as an actress the woman has no instincts. Actually, she just plain stinks—that maybe we should take all this to the police."

JB looked up from the program he was watching. "You mean turn Peter into the cops?"

"So, what would happen if we did? Would it be so terrible?"

It was intermission and Len had returned to his dressing room to have his makeup refreshed and change into his act three costume. JB hadn't watched the performance, he'd seen it often enough during rehearsals, but had instead been watching an episode of *LA Law* on the portable television Len kept in his dressing room.

"Well, first they would probably take Peter back to Bellevue and keep him there. Forever. Which would get no one anywhere close to working any of this mystery out. And then the police would probably end up charging us with withholding information concerning a murder. Which would get us, at the least, a large fine and possibly some jail time. The British call it perverting the course of justice."

"They do have a way with words, don't they?"

"And in the event the police did charge us, we wouldn't be able to seek or find our unknown recovering killer. Who, according to the rules of AA, you're not supposed to talk about anyway."

"Okay, I get the idea. Jeez, you're in a mood, aren't you? Who stuck a finger up your nose?"

"This guy out in Yonkers. He shot me down when I asked him for dinner."

"You were shot down?"

"Like a Messershmidt in World War II. Turns out he was straight, and I didn't see it."

"You?"

"In my defense it has been two months since I've been laid. It tends to fog the senses."

"That's understandable I guess. Two months

is like five in penis time. We could go out after the
show. You and I on the town. Maybe go to Marie's
Crisis. Could be fun."

"Yeah. Maybe. Let's do it."

CHAPTER 9

They had gone out after curtain as planned. They sang along with the piano at Marie's and ended up listening to Nancy LaMott at *Don't Tell Mama's* for her late show. The cab finally let them off at their apartment building at close to four.

When they got to his door JB asked, "Are you sleepy? I can make tea."

Len followed JB into his apartment. Spying a curled up and asleep Peter on his couch they both quietly went to the kitchen.

"What's he doing here?" Len asked. "I thought he was staying with his lover. What was his name?"

"Phan. Or The Dragon Queen. Whichever suits. But that's where I left him. At his place. I don't know why he's here. I guess I forgot to get my keys back, and he used them."

They heard a moan from the couch. Peter was obviously in the midst of a bad dream. He was rolling side to side and his hands were pushing away some demon or other. He was mumbling unintelligible words, punctuated with moans. The fear in the sounds was clear. Then, just as suddenly as it had started, he calmed and was sleeping soundly, clutching his pillow to his chest.

"Not having a good night is he?"

"Something's worrying him, that's for sure."

"Repressed memories maybe?"

"Not nice ones then. You know, I think I'm going to take him with me when I go back to Yonkers later today. I have the dead woman's lawyer's name and it might be interesting to see how Peter reacts."

"Besides, if he is this Nicholas person you found out about, then Yonkers should bring up a shitload of memories for him."

"That's what I'm counting on."

Peter was up before JB that morning. JB was awakened by him puttering in the kitchen. He checked the clock. It was ten. He'd had four and a half hours of sleep. Well, he was still young. He could get by on that.

He put his feet on the floor, rubbed the grit from his eyes, and went to the kitchen. Peter was standing there with a cup in his hands. The odor of coffee wafted to JB's nostrils.

"Do you have more of that?"

"It's instant. But the water is still hot."

"It will have to do."

As JB fixed his own cup he asked Peter why he had come back to his apartment the night before.

"Did I do wrong?"

"No, it's okay. I just thought you would stay with Phan at your own place."

"It didn't feel like I belonged there. That it was my house. The place just wasn't comfortable. And I hated the decorations. It was like being in a kung-fu movie. All that Chinese furniture. I felt out of place."

"Well, you can't deny you're a decorator, that's for sure. What about Phan. Didn't he make you feel at home?"

"He was the worst of it. He kept shoving these photo albums at me. As if it was incontrovertible proof I was his lover. He was pushing so hard. And he kept pawing at me. He seemed to be crazy intent on proving I belonged there. To the point where it started to get creepy. That's when I told him I wasn't staying. That I would talk to him when some of what's going on with me is cleared up. Then I came here."

"Well that's fine. But have a seat. There's something I need to talk to you about."

The ride out to Yonkers wasn't anywhere near as pleasant as the day before. Peter, who JB had eariler told about Nicholas—about another person he might be—was peppering JB with questions the whole way. He had taken the initial news quite calmly, then as he had thought about the

implications of it, what it might mean to his already murky life, anxiety had set in. He sat on the edge of his seat all the way out and kept coming up with point after point. Conundrum after conundrum. Who was this Nicholas? What did he have to do with him? Who was this Rosalie woman? And she's dead? Who killed her? Could it have been me? And on and on.

Unfortunately JB didn't have the solutions Peter was looking for. He had just as many questions as Peter did. If the dead woman was Peter's wife, why had he disappeared back in Nineteen-eighty? Debt? Another woman? Another man? If Peter had a wife how did Phan fit into the picture? And the biggie. Why would a sniper take out a seemingly innocent housewife in Yonkers of all places? Like dominos the questions just kept on piling up.

They got out at the Glenwood Station in Yonkers and went to the cab stand out front. JB gave the address of Rosalie's attorney to the driver and sat back. The cabby, a talkative sort, asked if they were new to Yonkers. "Just visiting," JB answered.

"Well, its a great city. You'll enjoy it here." He looked into his rearview mirror. "Say, you look like someone I know." He was talking to Peter.

Peter scooted up in his seat. "Really? I don't think I know you."

"But you ain't from here, so its unlikely. I was born and raised here myself. Hardly ever leave."

JB touched Peter on the shoulder. He scooted back on the seat to face him. "Do any of the streets or buildings around here ring any bells? You should be familiar with the area. That is if you grew up here."

The cabby looked into his mirror again.

Peter was looking out the window at the passing neighborhood. "Its like a movie I'm watching for the second time. You know what's coming, but not all the details."

"Well, familiarity might breed remembrance. Don't push for it. Let it come naturally. Oh, and when we get to the lawyers office..."

Peter turned to him.

"Let me do the talking. This man was Rosalie's attorney, not yours. He probably won't even know who you are. Or were. I think it might be best if we keep it like that. For the time being anyway."

"Okay. But won't he get suspicious when we start asking about this Nicholas person. You are going to do that, aren't you? I need to know about this guy, JB. I have to find out who he was. I..."

"I know Peter. And we'll find out as much as we can. Without raising more questions if we can help it."

The cab pulled up at a strip mall that consisted of five separate businesses. There was a sandwich shop, a launderette, a drug store, a barber shop, and the offices of Dodson Hines, attorney at law.

"Not exactly posh is it?"

JB had called ahead that morning and made an appointment so they went right to the door. The windows of the storefront were covered with a white paint on the inside. A simple sign made from dime store press-on black letters indicated the lawyers name. The door was a solid white block in a silver aluminum frame and it was locked. JB pressed the button at the side of the door and they were buzzed in.

Dodson Hines was not your old family retainer sort of lawyer. No oak paneled walls, no leather overstuffed furniture, no statues of ladies holding scales for this guy. He was obviously new—he'd probably passed the bar exam the week before—and young—he could have graduated from prep school the year before—and ambitious. He was a facsimile of the kid on *Family Ties,* Alex P. Keaton, but stubbier and rounder.

The office was spare. It had only a desk, a couple of chairs, and file cabinets lining the walls. It was all very utilitarian and cheap. Even his law degree, in a *Woolworth* plastic frame hung behind his desk, looked new and unused.

He stood and shook hands and got right down to business. Eager. "How can I help you..." He consulted his day planner. "...Mr. Bent, is it?" He smiled. He had dimples that made him look almost cherubic.

"I believe you are the attorney of record for the late Miss Rosalie Stymington. Is that correct?"

"Yes I am. In fact I filed her will at the court house just this morning. I'm her executor."

"Then I was wondering if I might ask some questions about the lady?"

"I offer a free consultation in my practice. Let's call it that. Okay?" His curiosity had been aroused. "As long as I'm not violating client privilege what is it you would like to know?"

"Well, since the lady is deceased that doesn't apply any longer, so let's start with how long had you been her lawyer?"

"Not all that long. She came to me a few months ago about another matter. But during that time she also retained me to draw up her will and put her affairs in order. And a good thing she did as it turns out."

"Right. But why would she do that? Did she think she was in some kind of danger? I ask because most people don't end up being killed by a sniper. Its very nature tends to make it a random act."

"No danger that I'm aware of. Its simply that until she came to my office her legal priorities hadn't included a will. Did you know most people don't write wills? They don't realize how important it can be. I was the one who suggested she make out hers.

Do you have a will, Mr. Bent?"

He wrote her will out all right. At a very substantial fee, JB was sure. "I've got it covered, thank you. This other matter she came to you about. Can you tell me what it was?"

He leaned back in his chair, knitted his hands, and put them under his chin. "I don't see why not. She had consulted me about having her late husband, Nicholas Bonanno, legally declared dead. He drowned in a fishing accident seven years ago and the statute of limitations allowed her to now pursue that end."

Peter started at this statement. He reached over and grabbed JB's arm. JB asked, "He hadn't already been declared dead?"

"When there's no body it takes seven years. That date was approaching. There was a matter of an insurance settlement involved."

"If I'm understanding you, her husband had an insurance policy that would pay out after he was officially deceased. Is that right?"

"Correct. She had continued paying the premiums on the policy since his accident to keep it in effect and now wanted to collect on it."

"For how much?"

"It was substantial. Near the million dollar mark."

"And now she's gone. Who collects now?"

"Since I filed the will this morning I suppose I can tell you. Its considered public knowledge now. She had no blood relatives, no children or siblings. Her parents were both deceased, so the bulk of the estate, after fees, of course, will go to her husband's uncle. A Mr. Sam Bonanno." Peter's grip on JB's arm tightened,

"That includes the house too?"

"And its contents."

"And the uncle is still alive."

"Living in New York City. I spoke with him yesterday."

JB got the address and phone number for the uncle and thanked Hines for his help. Peter and he then left the office and stood together in front of the sandwich shop.

"We're going to need another cab. We can have lunch while we wait." They went into the shop. JB called the cab company while Peter ordered them sandwiches at the counter.

"Where to next?" Peter asked when they sat down to eat.

"I want to go to the house. Look it over. How are you feeling? Have the memory banks started opening? You seemed to recognize the name of the uncle."

"I did. I remember him. Uncle Sam. He raised me after my parents died. Him and his wife, Ruth. But that's all. Its like I said. It all feels familiar, but that's the extent of it."

"Maybe the house will open the floodgates."

The cab, this time with a different driver, arrived and drove them to the Palisades area of town. Along a street lined with old trees that had trunks the size of oil drums, and uneven sidewalks where the roots had pushed the concrete slabs askew, there stood a row of original Nineteenth century houses. The driver pulled up. "This is Hudson Terrace. That's the place right there. At the corner."

"Thanks. Could you wait?" JB and Peter got out.

The Victorian mansion was painted white with green picking out the ornate gingerbread that characterized the style of the house. Sitting on a small rise on a corner lot a cast iron gate led to a set of steps leading up to the shaded wraparound porch.

Peter was excited. "Now this is really familiar. I grew up here. This was my house."

JB tried the gate and found it open. On the porch there was a crisscross of yellow crime scene police tape on the front door. It was locked. Peter had his hands up to his face looking into the front window. "That's the front parlor. With the dining room behind it. And behind that is the kitchen. Can we go in, JB?"

"Its all locked up. I don't think so."

"Wait. I know. Follow me." And Peter took off. JB followed him as he walked the porch around to the back of the house. He took a set of wooden stairs down into the back garden and then turned under the same stairs.

Peter went to a door and tried the knob. Then using a coin from his pocket he unscrewed the screen over the window that was set in at the top. He set aside the screen and then pushed up on the window. It opened a couple of inches, enough to let Peter reach in and unlock the door. "This is how I used to get back in when I'd sneak out as a teenager. I can't believe the window is still unlocked."

Peter took JB inside into a narrow boarded hallway with a basement off of one side and a laundry room off the other. "The kitchen is up there," and he led JB to another set of stairs at the other end of the hall. They climbed them and soon stood in the linoleum covered kitchen. The silence in the house was heavy. Whispering somehow seemed mandatory. "The living and dining rooms are through there," Peter hissed.

He left the kitchen and aimmed toward the front of the house. The living room, or front parlor, was decorated in the overstuffed and ornate style of the house's design and felt a lot like a period funeral home. Horsehair dark velvet covered furniture sat amidst crocheted lace covered tables studded with painted glass shaded lamps and knickknacks. A stuffed pheasant under a glass dome stared blindly out at the two men. The heavy lace curtains in the front window softened the afternoon light making it seem dour and gloomy inside. Peter pointed to the window nook. "That's where we set up the Christmas tree every year." Through a pair of sliding oak double doors a wooden balustered set of carpeted stairs led up to the next floors.

"My room was up there." And Peter was off again. JB followed him up. He wanted to see where the owner had died. That was on the widows walk on the third floor. He went up to the floor where two closed doors were on his left. Bedrooms. Probably maids rooms in the original house. Sheer curtained French doors on the right led out to the walk. JB opened them and stepped out. Wood floor, white railing. An attached flower box trailed ivy. There was a beautiful view of the river looking out from it.

On the left floor of the small balcony was a large dark blood stain soaked into the gray slatted wood. JB was standing where the woman had been shot only three days before. If she was hit in the head and fell back as the paper reported then the position of the stain indicated the fatal shot had to have come from his right. Along the street. From one of the trees? Had the sniper climbed up and waited until the woman had stepped out onto the walk? Then picked her off like a cherry on a sundae.

"JB, are you out here..." Peter stuck his head out the doors and looked toward him. Then he looked down at the blood stained floor. His face fell. His eyes widened, his jaw went slack. He began to moan—low at first, then it got louder. Panic overtook him as he pushed away from the doors and stumbled backward into the hallway.

JB went after him and found him crouched against the wall with his arms wrapped around his knees. He pointed at the French doors. "She was yelling. Screaming. 'Don't come near me. You're not supposed to be here. Get away.' I reached for her. Then she just dropped. Dead. Crumpled to the floor..."

He stood then and rushed toward the stairs.

"Peter. Wait." JB chased after him.

Peter turned back to JB. "I can't stay here. Get me out..."

When Peter was at the stairwell he took a backward step and finding empty space he stumbled. He fell down the stairs to the landing below and then, still trying to get away from whatever he was seeing, rolled down the next flight of stairs, stopping on that landing cringing and pulling into a ball.

JB knelt beside him and pulled him into his arms. "What is it, Peter? What are you seeing?"

The front door was slammed open by the foot of a uniformed cop. Next the cop was standing in the doorway, his gun drawn and turning from side to side. Then he looked up. He ran up the stairs to the landing where JB and Peter were crouched. Holding the weapon toward them he shouted, "Don't move." They didn't.

He was followed by another man, in plainclothes, who came up the stairs after him. He stood looking down at JB and Peter. Then he reached inside his coat and pulled out a badge. Showing it he announced, "Nicholas Bonanno, I am arresting you on suspicion of murdering Mrs. Rosalie Stymington Bonanno. You have the right to...."

While he read Peter his rights, the other cop put his gun away, pulled out a pair of cuffs, and grabbed Peter by the front of his jacket. He stood him up and closed the steel bracelets on his wrists, then led him down the stairs.

The plainclothes cop said to JB, "You're trespassing. This is a sealed crime scene. Get your ass out of here."

Then he turned and stomped out after Peter.

CHAPTER 10

He got outside just in time to watch Peter being driven off in a Yonkers police car. To the station house to be booked JB presumed. The cab they had arrived at the house in was still there, sitting at the curb. JB asked the driver to wait a few more minutes. Then he turned and walked down the street.

He was pretty sure the police had made a mistake in arresting Peter, or Nicholas—whichever he was. It didn't make sense that he could have done it with what JB knew of the case so far. For one thing, according to Tony Kilbreth, the newspaper reporter, the woman was shot from a distance and not close up. He said they hadn't found any shell casings at the scene. Of course, they could have been picked up and taken by the shooter. That would have been the professional thing to do. But Peter, in his panicked reaction to the scene upstairs, said she had just dropped and was dead. That would have been in front of him. If she had been shot close up there would have been a completely different set of stain marks on the floor of the widows walk.

JB turned and looked back at the house. He was calculating how high and how far away the sniper would have had to be to make the fatal killshot. He was two trees down from the iron gate leading to the house. In front of the next door neighbors house. That tree had a fork about five feet up from the ground. If someone was to stand in that fork he would have a clear view of the house. JB pulled himself up and stood in the crook of the tree. Sure enough at shoulder height on a left sweeping branch there was a white spot where something had rubbed the bark off the tree—like a gun barrel?— also over to the right there was a small black round spot where someone had crushed out a cigarette.

He leaped down to the ground and looked around. There were several cigarette butts scattered on the ground at the trunk. He picked one up. It was crushed and burnt but the filter and some of the white paper was left. There was tiny printing on the paper. JB straightened out the wrinkled butt. The writing wasn't in English. There was an apostrophe and another odd mark over the letters, and the filter had a dark brown band around it. It couldn't be anything but foreign. Turkish maybe? At any rate it wasn't what you would find under a tree in the city of Yonkers. Not normal. A *Pall Mall* or a *Winston* would be normal. JB took a page out of his day planner, folded it in half, and put two more of the butts in it. He closed it and stored the package in his backpack. Then he looked around.

This was a neighborhood. How was that no one heard a gun shot when the woman was killed? He went over to the gate of the house in front of the tree. On the porch there was a pile of newspapers. Several days worth. JB opened the mailbox by the gate. It was stuffed with unpicked up mail. The neighbors must be away. And maybe the shooter had used a silencer? That would explain the lack of noise.

Then he went back to the cab.

JB arrived in front of the police station and got out intending to go inside and do some basic mad queen yelling. What the hell were they thinking? Peter, or Nicholas, whichever they were choosing to call him, could not have killed. Period. JB didn't think he had it in him. Unless the person he was before the bump to his head and the amnesia was a total psychopath. Was he? He would have to check with Phan. He would know if his lover was a nutjob or not. And, on top of that, the police had to have their facts wrong. It was JB's intention to point that out in no uncertain terms.

JB started up the steps to the entrance when the front door opened and Tony Kilbreth came out. The newspaper man was writing in a notebook and not seeing JB at all. JB stepped aside and grabbed Tony's shoulder.

"What?" He started and turned to face JB. His

hand came up and brushed at his coat. "Oh, Mr. Bent. You are a touchy freely kind of guy aren't you?"

"Just trying to get your attention."

"Well, what can I do for you? I'm kinda in a hurry."

"You're writing about them..." He jerked a thumb at the station. "...arresting Nicholas Bonanno aren't you? He's a friend of mine. What have you found out?"

"Yes I am. What a story. Missing husband comes back from the dead to kill his long-suffering wife."

"Are you sure that's what happened?"

"You aren't? Why?"

"Better I should ask you why they think he did it?"

"Turning up after being missing for seven years seems pretty suspicious, don't you think?"

"How did they know he was at the house? They burst in like Godzilla attacking Tokyo."

"A cabby that drove him to a lawyers office this morning recognized him. They went to high school together. He called the police."

"Then him being still alive is all they have on him. That isn't enough to hold him."

"Also since they arrested him they took his fingerprints. That gave them even more reason."

"What?"

"His prints matched some unknowns found at the house where the woman was shot."

"All that proves is he's been inside the house. Hell, even I've done that."

"They found them the day after the murder."

"Oh. Well, okay then. But I'm still not convinced. What was his motive?"

"The insurance money. He wanted a share, she refused, they argued, he killed her. Open and shut according to the cops."

"Not very original…"

"It was a lot of money. Anyway, they're holding him until they can get him into court."

"When?"

Tony had started walking again, aiming for the newspaper office to write his story. JB walked swiftly to catch up.

"When's he going to court?"

"The judge is away. Not until next Monday."

That meant he had only days to get this all worked out. JB took off in the opposite direction, headed for the train station. He had to get back to the city. Quickly.

There he could go to see Nicholas' uncle. He was the person who took over raising the boy when he was a child alone. He must have some feelings for his now newly arisen nephew and might help him in his predicament.

CHAPTER 11

W hen JB got back to the city he went straight home intending to call up Peter's/Nicholas' uncle and arrange a meeting. Instead he bypassed his own place and went up to Len's apartment. He tapped the brass knocker.

Len answered almost immediantly, as if he was standing just on the other side of the door.

"That was quick."

"I just got in. I was hanging up my coat. Come on in. I have some news."

"So do I."

They settled on the couch.

"I just got back from a meeting. The one where I heard the guy confess."

"And?"

"I showed the sketch around and only a couple of people remembered him, although one woman wants to meet him if he isn't married."

"You've gone into the matchmaking business?"

"Only in my own self interest. Anyway, no one had seen the guy at that meeting again, but one lady said she'd seen him over at Fireside. That's a meeting on the Westside at the Y.M.C.A. there. I'm going to go tomorrow."

JB reached into his backpack and took out the folded paper he'd stashed in it. "I found these near the house in Yonkers. I think they were smoked by the sniper. Your guy. Do you remember if he smoked?"

"He did. Like a Mississippi smokehouse."

"Do you remember if the cigarettes were like these? Take a look. They aren't a standard American brand."

Len picked one of the butts up and examined it. "Definitely not American. The filter with the brown band on it is totally different. What makes you think these are his?"

"I figured out where the shooter had taken his shot from to kill the woman. It was a tree with a clear view of the widow's walk. These were lying at the base of the tree." JB leaned forward and pointed. "And in addition to the band there's this printing."

Len looked again. "I see what you mean. Can I take one of these? I can check with my old tobacconist and try to find out where he might have bought them. The neighborhood smoke shops wouldn't carry these."

"My thinking too. And we really do have to find this guy..." JB went on to tell Len about Peter being arrested. Then he had to fill him in on the whole Nicholas persona as why he was a suspect in the first place. "...so we have to find the real killer or Peter—I mean Nicholas—is going to end up in the gas chamber at Sing Sing."

"Does he have to stay in jail? What about bail?"

"The local judge is out of town so he won't even get arraigned until next week. Bail wouldn't be set until then. Meanwhile, I'm going to get in touch with his uncle and see if he'll help." That occasioned more explaining as to who the uncle was and what was his place in the scheme of things. "Also, I want to talk to Phan again. Either one of them will come to Peter's aid. I'm sure of it."

The two separated when Len left to go to the theater and its eight-thirty curtain. JB, finally back in his own apartment, got on the phone. First he called Phan.

He was at home, which meant JB had to explain why he was calling. That Peter had been arrested and was in a Yonkers jail. Phan was ready to get on a train right that moment, but JB told him it would do no good. It would be better to wait until morning. Then there would be normal visiting hours and Peter—or Nicholas—could see any visitors then.

"But I am wondering if you could come over this evening," Phan asked. "There is questions I have."

That fit right in with JB's plans. There were some questions he wanted to ask himself. "Sure. I can be there in about an hour. Is that all right."

"That is good."

Then JB tried the number he had gotten for Peter/Nicholas' uncle. JB guessed he would have to get used to calling Peter by the name Nicholas from now on. He couldn't keep adding a slash every time he said the man's name. And it looked like Nicholas was indeed his birth name. So Nicholas it would have to be from that moment on.

The phone had rung five or six times before an answering machine picked up. JB hung up not wanting to leave a message such as his on a mechanical device. In person was called for in these circumstances. He would have to try again in the morning.

JB took the subway down to Phan's neighborhood and then walked the rest of the way to his business-slash-apartment. God, there he was again with the slash thing. He rang the bell, and waited for Phan to answer.

JB could see through the glass door the shadowed form of the kimono clad Phan descending the stairs and wafting his way across the office. He was like a spirit in a fairy story told to scare small children. He opened the door and smiled. Except it didn't seem to be such a friendly smile. It was more cunning than hospitable. JB shivered. No wonder Nicholas hadn't wanted to stay overnight with this guy. He was like something out of a Sax Rohmer Fu Manchu mystery story. With an opium den and sex slaves in a torture room in the back. JB shook himself. Get over it, kiddo. Who's being the drama queen now?

"Come in, JB." If he had added 'Let me stick flaming bamboo shoots under your fingernails' JB wouldn't have been surprised. He stepped in. "Upstairs, please."

JB headed for the stairs with Phan following.

"I have tea prepared. Or would you prefer sake?" he asked once they were settled in the living room. JB on the couch. Phan kneeling on the floor. This guy has seen *Flower Drum Song* one too many times, was what JB was thinking.

"Uh, do you have a soda? That would be just fine."

Phan nodded, slid upward and went to the kitchen. JB noticed a stack of photo albums on the low coffee table in front of him. Nicholas had said that Phan had insisted on showing him photos of the two of them. JB picked an album up and opened it. Black pages with snapshots carefully lined up in two rows. Nicholas and Phan on their vacations. The two of them under a sign that said *Welcome to Nantucket.* Arms entwined on the dock at Fire Island. Under the tree at Rockefeller Center at Christmas time.

Phan was back and handed over the can of soda and a glass. He indicated the album. "Our life together. But Peter did not remember it. It is sad. So much time to disappear."

"It's all inside his head. It's just locked away in a sort of file cabinet right now. He'll find the key eventually and it will all come back. But there is something I have to tell you."

"Ah, yes. His being arrested. Why is this? Why is he in prison?"

"Well, brace yourself, Phan. It's beginning to look like Peter is not who you think he is. There is ample evidence to support the fact that his real name is Nicholas Bonanno. And he's being accused of the murder of a woman named Rosalie Stymington of Yonkers. That was her maiden name. She was his wife until he disappeared seven years ago and apparently began living with you as Peter Sterling here in New York. And now he's being accused of murdering her."

JB braced himself. Here it comes, the whole operatic over-the-top reaction. JB was ready to call the paramedics if needs be. But Phan surprised him. He remained calm. As if he knew already. That it was no great surprise. "It is impossible," he declared. "My Peter is a gentle man. There is no violence such as this in him." Well, that answered the was he a psychopath question.

"So, what do you think?" JB sat back, tipping the photo album still on his lap. A picture slid out from one of the pages. JB picked it up meaning to put it back in the album, instead he held on to it while Phan spoke.

"I think it explains very much. Peter was always distant. He kept a piece of himself away from me. In a place I wasn't allowed. He never gave information about his past. He was very...secretive? Is that right?"

"That's right. So he wouldn't tell you about his past?"

"Some of his youth. Bits and pieces. A story here. A anecdote there. Nothing at all about right before he met me. But a man's memories are his own. I did not pry."

So Nicholas had always been vague about his past. His memory had been tattered long before this latest incident on the streets of the Village. JB began to wonder what had happened to him on that fishing trip he was on seven years ago. That seemed to be the starting point for most everything that came after. Before that it had all been pretty normal. But after arriving in New York, his meeting Phan, and being vague about what had come before—well, that was the anomaly. And then forgetting all about Phan after his recent mugging. Was there such a thing as double amnesia? Could a memory be lost twice?

JB glanced at the picture in his hand. "Well,

you must have had a fun life together." He held out the picture. "You look great in drag, Phan. So real. Was this Halloween?" The picture showed a woman and a masked man. He was in an Army dress uniform, she was in a garment called an Ao Dai, the traditional Vietnamese woman's dress. JB assumed it was Phan and Nicholas at a party of some sort.

Phan leaned in, then took the picture from JB's hand. "That is not me and Peter. That is my sister with a man at the place where she worked. A party. In Saigon. Before we come to USA."

"Oh, I didn't know you had a sister."

"And a brother. He's here in New York. She is dead. Killed during the war."

And she was also a bar girl if the picture was any indication. And the man with her was probably a random trick. "She was very pretty. You do look very much like her."

"She was most beautiful. And died a useless death."

"As did so many in that war."

Phan nodded, ran his hand over the picture and slipped it away inside his kimono. "Now, what can we do to help my partner?"

JB told him when Nicholas would be arraigned and that bail would be set then. Then he handed over the card from the lawyers office in Yonkers. "He should be able to help you. Call him next week first thing."

Phan said he would and JB left.

The next day Len was up early. At least early for him. Since final curtain was at eleven fifteen every night he seldom got home before one or two in the morning. So ten was early on his clock.

He got dressed to go out because he was going to hit Fifth Avenue to see a tobacconist there who he knew sold exotic brands of cigarettes. He wanted to show him the butt JB had picked up in Yonkers. Maybe he could identify the brand. If he could it would help in ferreting out the assassin he was looking for.

The shop was redolent with the fumes from cigars, cigarettes and various blends of pipe tobacco, making Len's mouth water. He had been a smoker in his drinking days, but with sobriety came a wish to rid himself of several of his bad habits. Booze and nicotine were first, caffeine was next on the list.

He showed the butts to the clerk and was told that the brand was Asian, not carried there, and he should probably try down in Chinatown. So Len headed for Canal Street and the edges of the district. He found a smoke shop near Pearl Paints and went in. The man behind the counter was reading a newspaper printed in the hieroglyphs of Chinese. Rows of print running up and down instead of back and forth.

The owner looked up, then stood. "I can help?" he said, and he bowed slightly. Len wasn't sure if the accent and the manner was real or put on for the tourists. But then, what matter?

Len put the cigarette butt on the counter. "Can you tell me what brand this is from the butt? I thought the brown band might make it easy to know it?"

The man leaned over. Then looked up. "This Vietnamese brand. See. Name on paper. Tôt Hoa Lá. Means Fine Flower Leaf. Good brand. Very strong."

"Do you sell these?"

"Sure. Only store in Chinatown that does. You want some?"

"Yes please. I'll buy a pack. Also I was wondering if you know this man?" Len pulled out the sketch Jerome had made.

The man laid a pack of the cigarettes on the counter. The paper package was white with a chrysanthemum in yellow and the name arched over the flower on the label. The owner peered at the picture. "Sure. He buy these." He tapped his finger on the paper wrapped cigarettes. "Come here to get them."

"Do you know his name?"

"No, he's a customer only. See him once in a while."

"Well thank you. How much do I owe you?"

The noon meeting at Fireside was already in progress when Len arrived. This particular meeting was called Fireside because the space the Y.M.C.A. had assigned this AA group actually had a carved stone fireplace in it. The room was long and narrow with tall mullioned windows at the far end. Metal folding chairs were set up in three rows facing the speakers table with the red and white printed cloth lists of the twelve steps flanking it. The speaker had just begun so Len took a seat at the back and waited for the break. After the qualifier was finished the meeting would adjourn for ten minutes then would commence again with sharing from the members.

Members crowded at the coffee table or broke into pairs while Len asked around and showed the sketch of the man he was looking for. A couple of people said they had seen him but not at this meeting. He was at the later meeting. The one that convened at four. That meant Len would have to hang around the Westside all afternoon so he could find this guy. What the hell was he going to do for those several hours until the next meeting? Twiddle his thumbs?

Then the meeting was called back to order and Len again took his seat at the back. That's when one of the most handsome men he'd seen in eons sat down next to him. The word beautiful, if it could be applied to a man—and in this case it did—came instantly to mind. The guy looked like he had stepped out of a magazine ad, which made sense, since he had to be a model. In a whisper he introduced himself.

"Hi. I'm Gary P."

"I'm Len. Len M."

"I know who you are. Would you like to go for coffee after the meeting?"

Maybe he wouldn't have to twiddle after all. At least not his thumbs.

When JB finally got a hold of Sam Bonanno, the uncle had just returned from going to Yonkers to see Nicholas. Which relieved JB of having to shock him with the news that his long deceased nephew wasn't dead after all. The Yonkers police had called and informed Sam of Nicholas' existence and arrest. Small towns, JB remembered, knew all of the facts about their citizens. They had undoubtedly known Nicholas' uncle's address and phone in New York and informed him. Sam and JB arranged to meet at Sam's apartment in an hour and hash out what needed to be done for Nicholas.

JB had found the Park Avenue address with no trouble and was admiring the unit when Sam said, "Nickola told me you had been helping him. I really appreciate your being there for him. This is a real mess isn't it?"

Calling him Nickola was an indication for JB of

how long and deep the relationship was between the man and his new friend up in Yonkers. They had to have been intimates for some time for Sam to use the familiar diminutive as he did. It was also a very Italian form of address. Old country and charming.

Sam Bonanno was older than JB by maybe fifteen or so years. In his late-fifties at any rate. With the standard pot belly, gray temples, and tortoise shell framed bifocals that go along with the age. His resemblance to Nicholas was uncanny. They could have been twins, separated by twenty years of course, but certainly from the same seed. And Sam appeared to be a kindly man. Similar in disposition to Nicholas. His concern for his newly rediscovered nephew was obvious. He was then telling JB how Nicholas came into his life as a boy of fourteen. How he and his now deceased wife had become his guardians after his parents died, and how they had moved stock and barrel to Yonkers, where they ran the hotel for the five years Nicholas was growing and then drafted into the Army. Most of it JB had gleaned from the bits and pieces Nicholas had been able to remember and from the newspaper accounts he'd read only the day before.

Then Sam was telling about the day Nicholas had disappeared back in Nineteen-eighty. He had gone out on the Hudson River in a borrowed boat for some fishing. A rainstorm had come up, squalls must have overtaken the boat, and Nicholas was gone. Swept overboard it was presumed. Two days later they found the boat overturned on the shore about thirty miles downstream from where he started with no sign of Nicholas anywhere. The police called it an accidental drowning, but without a body the estate was thrown into limbo. Rosalie, Nicholas' wife, had stayed in the house but closed the hotel after he was gone. She took back her maiden name because it was her father who had kept her going after her husband's disappearance. Supporting her even after his own death three years later of a stroke. And now for Nicholas to turn up all these years later. "It is a miracle, is it not?" Sam clapped his hands together.

"Do you know the whole story of our meeting?" JB asked

"Only what Nickola told me this morning."

"Then it definitely is Nicholas Bonanno? The Nickola you met in Yonkers is neither an imposter or a doppelganger?"

"Yes, of course. Was there any doubt?"

"A great deal to be honest. Let me tell you the circumstances under which we met?"

"Please."

So JB began with their meeting at the Gay Community Center and then went on with what their subsequent search and investigation had so far brought to light. Nicholas' apparent second life as Peter Sterling. His successful interior design business there in Manhattan. His lover Phan.

"Wait. You're saying that Nickola is a homosexual?" Sam looked absolutely shocked. Shit. JB had just told the man something he didn't know yet about his nephew. That could be uncomfortable.

"That's right. At least he's been living with another man for the last seven years. I think they would have been intimate somewhere along the line."

"I'm so surprised. Nickola was never like that before. He was a good church going boy. I never suspected he might be a queer."

For all of New York City's supposed liberal attitudes toward gays there were still pockets of homophobic prejudice everywhere. From subtle job discrimination to fire bombs thrown at gay bars it was rampant in the city. Men were killed for even being suspected of a limp wrist. You could turn on Phil Donahue any day of the week and see homophobia paraded proudly. Name calling, vile disparagement, blatant disdain shouted proudly by an audience from the broughs around the city. Nobody could hate like a Long Island housewife.

"Sam, be glad Nicholas found someone to help him. If he hadn't found Phan he would have been a walking target. His partner saved him. Literally saved his life, Sam."

Sam nodded, still trying to wrap his own feelings around this new information. He became quiet again as JB continued with his report. He told him everything they had found so far. How they had come to go out to Yonkers in the first place and how the police had burst in and arrested Nicholas. JB even included Len's tale of a sniper trying to get sober and regretting his unlawful profession. It was all tied together in some odd fashion. JB just hadn't unraveled it all yet. It was like a ball of last years Christmas lights.

Sam shook his head. "Poor Rosalie. Being cut down like that. She was a nice young woman. The police have no real motive for her being shot, do they?"

JB had been slightly taken aback at the news that Nicholas was married. Not that homosexual men didn't get married all the time. To meet family expectations, to stay in their closets. But to abandon a wife in one city to begin an affair with a man in another was out of the norm. Nicholas didn't seem the type to shirk such a responsibility. Then again he was suffering from amnesia and had lost his past. That would include Rosalie. JB told Sam of his talk with Tony the Yonkers newspaper man and what he had proposed as the motive the police were working with. The money.

"But that's preposterous. Nicholas and Rosalie were very much in love. Look." He went to a set of wooden shelves and picked up a framed picture. "This was taken on their wedding day. Look at the way they're looking at each other. Love in bloom. Right?"

JB stood and went to where Sam was standing. He looked at the picture and had to agree. The couple in the picture seemed very much in love. But it was their wedding day. Doesn't everyone look happy in wedding photos? Who knew what happened after the fairy tale ended? Were Snow White and the Prince a happy couple? Or was he a spoiled abusive lout who always resented her living with seven little people? "So they were married in Nineteen-seventy-four?"

"That's right. Just after he got out of the hospital. He and Rosalie were high-school sweethearts. She'd waited for him while he was away."

"Hospital?"

"He was in Vietnam. Wounded in a bomb blast and sent back." Sam turned back to the shelves and picked up another picture. This one was a formal portrait of Nicholas in his Army uniform. "He got a Purple Heart." Sam showed that to him too.

"How long was he over there?" JB asked.

"He was drafted in Nineteen-seventy. Right out of high school. We wanted him to go to Canada. He had friends there from when his father was stationed with the American embassy. There were a lot of young men who went to Canada back then. But he wouldn't go. He reported to the Army like the up right boy that he was. He was sent over to Vietnam straight out of boot camp. In seventy-one. Stationed in Saigon. And then sent back, with a wounded leg, in seventy-three."

JB leaned in to look at the other pictures on the Nicholas shelf. Sam had created a sort of shrine to honor his thought dead nephew. He'd filled it with high school trophies, framed pictures, and other paraphernalia from his life up to his disappearance. JB noticed a snapshot from Nicholas' Vietnam years. It was of him in his everyday fatigues standing with another man. They had their arms slung over each other's shoulders and were smiling into the camera. They were holding up rifles in their other hands. The sort of picture thousands of vets had sent back home during the era. JB picked it up and looked closer.

It was the other man standing with Nicholas that JB was looking at. He was blond, taller than Nicholas, a bit thinner, and looked for all the world like GI Joe. JB could swear it was Len's sniper. He was sure of it.

"Who's this?" JB held out the picture to Sam.

Sam looked and said, "That's Dick somebody or other. I don't remember his last name. He was a friend of Nickola's. Why?"

Rhymes with Wick Len had said. JB explained who this was and showed Sam the sketch that Len and Jerome had produced. "I think this guy in the picture and my friend Len's sniper are the same person. The person who confessed to killing Rosalie was a friend of Nicholas'. Oh, man. This can either get him in more trouble or get him out of jail. I'm not sure which."

"What do you mean?"

"If this Dick guy was the sniper, the actual killer, then it exonerates Nicholas of Rosalie's murder, and he's free of the charges against him."

"That's wonderful. We have to find this Dick person right away."

"But..."

"What?"

"What if it turns out that Nicholas hired this guy he previously knew to kill his wife? That would put him right in the middle of a conspiracy to commit murder. That would be disastrous."

"Then we shouldn't find this man?"

"Sam, I think we have to. Regardless of what it portends for Nicholas. The man is a killer for hire. He has to be stopped."

Star fuckers. Gotta love em.

Len was smiling to himself as he turned on West Sixty-third Street and headed for the four o'clock meeting at the "Y". Gary P. had turned out to be a very agreeable way to spend the afternoon. He was, if nothing else, enthusiastic in his love making, and nicely affectionate after. Unfortunately, he was also dumb as a board. Len was pretty sure he spelled fellatio with a six. It was often the curse of very good looking men. His sole purpose in asking Len for coffee was to get him into bed so he'd have something to brag about later at the bar. Len had been willing to oblige.

An arm reached out from the side of the double columned vestibule entrance to the "Y". It went around Len's neck and pulled him into the darkened area at the side of the doors. Len could feel the body of his attacker pressed against his back. He felt his hot breath near his ear, and it wasn't nearly as pleasant a sensation as it had been an hour eariler. It reeked of stale coffee and old tobacco. "I hear you've been looking for me," the voice said angrily.

Len choked out, "I would have to know who you are to answer that."

The arm at his neck loosened. Len stepped away and turned. He was facing Dick the AA sniper. Damn, he'd finally caught up with the guy.

And Dick didn't look happy as he pulled out a cigarette pack, tapped one out, and lit it. Len noticed the filter had a brown band around it. The

Vietnamese brand he had found that morning. Len figured the man was pissed because Len was sticking his nose into this obviously suspicious and very touchy man's business. And he wanted to know why? Since Len didn't want to be another notch on the sniper's gun sight what the hell did he do? Deflect the man's aim, right? Make him think Len's looking for him was innocent.

He was taller than Len remembered. And burly. Not out of shape, but broad and narrow in all the right places. You could probably do laundry on his abs. Definitely ex-military. Green Beret even. With the expected iron jaw and steely eyed expression. He looked to be able to make origami folded birds out of Len's pelvis if he was angered. He would have to tread gingerly.

Dick blew a stream of smoke. "Now, what do you want with me. I don't know you." Then he looked puzzled. "But you look familiar."

"You've probably seen me on TV. I act."

"So what's that to me?"

"Nothing. Just context."

"Context, huh. Well, back off, buddy. I don't need anybody lookin' for me." He poked Len on the chest. "You should leave me the hell alone."

Len smiled what he hoped was ingratiatingly. "I saw you at a meeting a few days ago and you seemed to be in some distress. Dick wasn't it. I'm Len M. I have ten months so far. I was hoping you were all right now. Are you?"

Dick relaxed a bit, thinking Len was simply another AA person concerned with his sobriety. "I haven't had a drink in four days. It's hell, but I guess I'm okay."

"No. You're a winner. We do it one day at a time, right?"

"Right. But I have a sponsor already. That's been a big help. He's going to be at this meeting.

I'm supposed to meet him."

"Great. That's the way to work the program. How is that job problem you mentioned? What did you do about that? What was it again?"

Dick was wary. "I'm in the rubbage business," he said slowly. "I get rid of unwanted riff-raff."

"Ah, a sanitation engineer then?" Len laughed neverously. It was a stretch but from a very oblique angle it would wash as a metaphor for hired killer.

"In a manner of speaking."

Another man came into the vestibule and stopped. "Dick? Are you coming to the meeting?"

They both turned. Standing there was an older man in jeans and sneakers.

Dick said, "My sponsor." He spoke to the man, "I'm coming Bill. I'll be right with you." Then to Len, "Hey, thanks for your concern. I'll see you around. Okay?"

"You got it. It only works if you work it, right?" Len smiled and waved him off. He and the other man walked into the building. Len took a deep breath. Had he got away with it? He wasn't dead or maimed, so maybe.

Len waited a moment and then followed. He stopped at the bank of pay phones in the lobby, put in his quarter, and dialed JB's number. He got his machine.

"JB, this is Len. The sniper guy is here at Fireside. The meeting just started so he'll be here another hour. Get over here when you get this message. I'll be in the meeting."

CHAPTER 12

Sam and JB arrived at the Westside "Y" about sixty-five minutes after Len's message was left on the machine. It was only luck that had caused JB to check his messages to begin with. Usually he got his messages when he got home after being out. But Sam had an appointment with his lawyer concerning Nicholas and wanted JB to come along.

Since he wouldn't be getting home until late he used the code to access his machine from Sam's.

Sam paid the cab while JB headed inside the "Y". He looked around the vaguely Gothic lobby and then headed for the back where he saw a group of people standing. The AA meeting was just breaking up. He'd missed his opportunity. JB could see Len with another man just outside the brown rod iron studded medieval looking doors. He went up to them after waiting for Sam to catch up.

"Sorry I'm late, Len. I only just got your message."

"And the guy isn't here anymore, JB. I lost him again. He skipped out at the break, I guess. This is Bill. His sponsor. I was just filling him in on what we suspect." Len finished with his explanation. Bill shook his head.

"I thought there must be something else bothering Dick. Since he was so new I kept telling him to focus on getting sober. That he could deal with whatever else there was later."

"And that's what you're supposed to do, Bill. You didn't do anything wrong."

JB said, "You talk to him every day, right? Well, has he said where he's staying? Maybe we can catch him at his place."

Bill thought a moment. "I think he said he was staying here. At the "Y". Until he can find a place that's cheaper." Like a hotel the "Y" had several floors of rooms they rented by the night. Everyone knew that. Even the Village People sang about it.

"Do you know Dick's last name? He'd be registered under his last name."

"I can't give you his last name. It's part of the program."

Len spoke up. "Under the circumstances— considering the laws he's broken—I think you can give it, Bill. You don't want to be responsible for his doing it again do you?"

It was a dilemma. How did he keep his word to remain anonymous and still give up the miscreant. Bill considered it for a moment and then told the three men to follow him. They did—to the registration desk. Bill told them to stay back while he went up to the desk and spoke with the clerk. A few minutes later he came back to the group. "He's in room two-oh-four. But you don't have access to the floors with rooms. You have to have a passkey."

Len hesitated only a moment. He went to the desk himself. He was soon back and holding up a key. "Who says we can't get onto the floors. I'm in room two-thirty-three. Same floor at least."

They thanked Bill, he said good bye, and the three of them, JB, Len, and Sam, headed for the elevators.

On the correct floor they started checking numbers. Before they found 204 Sam brought up a salient point. Exactly what were they going to do once they found this person? They had no authority to arrest him. They only had suspicions that he was the one who had killed Rosalie. And did they really want to confront a stone cold killer? Was this a prudent thing to do? Wouldn't it be more sensible to call the police?

At the correct door Len knocked. "We'll play it by ear. I talked to him already, so I'll do the talking now. You two stand back." There wasn't an answer so Len knocked again. "Hello," he said. "Are you there, Dick?" Still no answer. Len tried the doorknob. It was unlocked. He opened it and looked in. "I think maybe the cops were a better idea after all."

He stood back as JB stepped up and looked in. Dick the AA sniper was lying on his back on a blood soaked bedspread on the lower bunk bed staring blankly at the bottom of the bunk above.

He was quite dead.

"Oh, shit."

Sam looked over JB's shoulder. "Now we have to call the police."

"Who we have to call is the desk downstairs. Let them take care of it." JB thought a moment. "But wait on that. He's not going anywhere, and waiting will give us a chance to check out his stuff. Maybe there'll be a clue to Rosalie's killing. If Nicholas is involved in it you'd want to know, right Sam?"

The search wasn't hard. The room only had the set of bunk beds, a table with a TV, and a chair. There was also a free standing wooden closet beside the door. Narrow and cramped the room couldn't have held much more. The table drawer didn't have any papers in it, the top only held a copy of The Big Book—the AA Bible—along with some empty writing paper, a lamp and the TV. JB picked up the book and flipped through it. There was writing on several of the back pages. Dick's cramped handwriting covered four or five of the blanks left at the back of the book.

"What do you make of this, Len?"

He looked. "I'll bet he was starting a personal inventory. It's one of the twelve steps."

Desecrating books wasn't JB's regular practice but he wanted to read what Dick had written, and there wasn't going to be time right then. His "inventory" might hold a clue. He tore the pages from the book, folded them, and put them in his backpack.

The closet was where Dick had stored his few clothes. A couple pairs of jeans and two shirts on hangers. One pair of sneakers on the bottom shelf. Underwear and socks neatly folded on the top shelf. All in squared up for inspection shape. A remnant from his Army days probably. There were no real personal items except for a shaving kit and that held only the expected. Toothbrush, razor, deodorant.

JB stood up and swept the room again with his eyes. "He doesn't have much does he? You'd think being a hired killer would pay better wouldn't you?"

"Can we get out of here, JB?" Len crossed his arms. "His eyes are just staring. It's creepy. Besides he's starting to smell." The odor of excrement was filling the air. In death his sphincter had let go.

"Where's he looking?" JB bent down so he was level with the body. He looked in the same direction as the corpse's staring eyes. He wasn't actually staring up at the bottom of the bunk but rather at the closet. Or the top of it. JB grabbed the chair and carried it over. He stood on it and looked at the top. Set at the back was a black leather hard-shell suitcase.

"What's this?" JB lifted it down, grunting as he did.

"You know there's a gym downstairs, JB. Maybe you should get in a workout."

He laid the bag on the desk. The suitcase was pretty beat up and when opened, empty.

"It's awfully heavy for being an empty piece of luggage."

JB ran his fingers along the bottom of the case, then under the cardboard fabric covered bottom. He lifted.

"Whoa. What's this?"

The bottom of the suitcase contained a rifle. It was broken down with the pieces individually wrapped in white cloth. Each piece was set in a custom cut foam space so they wouldn't rattle around when carried. This was highly professional stuff. This was a clean, well oiled, killer of a gun.

Sam looked at the pieces. "That's a Remington. Top of the line. But its been altered so it will break down easily. The barrels been cut too. And look at that sight." Sam reached to pick it up.

JB stopped him. "Careful. Fingerprints."

He picked it up with the wrapping cloth still on it and looked through the lens. "This is really one superior weapon. Reliable. And adapted for distance. This is one hell of a scope. Accurate at long distances, I'll bet."

"It's also damn good proof that he's the sniper we've been looking for. I'll bet this gun matches the bullets that killed Rosalie Stymington."

"That means that Nicholas didn't do it. He'll be free."

"I don't understand why there aren't any personal items here. Papers. Phone numbers. There's nothing."

"Maybe he didn't think the room was safe. He kept them someplace else."

"Check his pockets. Len. Is there a key?"

"I'm not touching him, JB."

"For Christ's sake, Len. It's just a dead body, not the boogy man." JB bent and went through the man's pockets. He found a key on an elastic band. A Y.M.C.A. gym key for one of their lockers. "This is what I was looking for. You can call the desk now."

JB left Len and Sam to deal with the desk, the death and its aftermath, and the police who were sure to follow like Mary's lambs.

He made his way by elevator down to the second floor and the locker rooms of the gym. Beige painted lockers, carpeted concrete, wooden benches, and a smell similar to the inside of a wet Russian wrestler's jockstrap was what he found. He checked the number on the metal tag attached to the elastic and quickly, by going up and down the rows, found the right locker.

Inside were gym clothes and a cheap paper expandable file folder. JB took the folder, stored it in his backpack, and left the locker room to go to the lobby where he was going to join up with his friends.

Except they weren't there. He wandered about and looked in all the open areas and they hadn't got to the lobby yet. And he was stuck there.

He couldn't go back upstairs because he didn't have a pass key. He couldn't just abandon them by going home. So what was he to do? Then he remembered Len carried his mobile phone. It was a clunky heavy brick of a phone, but it meant JB could find out what was up. He headed for the bank of public phones.

Len picked up and said "Hello?"

"It's JB. Where are you?"

"Oh, Dave, I meant to call you..."

"Dave? No, it's JB."

Len spoke to someone else. "It's Letterman. I was supposed to do his show tonight." Then he was back on the phone. "I'm sorry Dave, but I can't do the show now. I'm much too busy."

"And you're a nutcase. I'm guessing that the cops are there."

"That's right."

"So, I shouldn't wait for you and Sam?"

"Right again."

"Okay, I'll go on home. Meet me when you can."

"Will do. As soon as I can arrange it."

Len arrived about twenty minutes after JB got home. JB was still in the preparation stages of getting tea together. Putting the kettle on, gathering cups, filling the sugar bowl, finding spoons, putting cookies on a plate...

He had meant to sit and go through Dick's file folder while he drank his tea, but Len's arrival put the plan on hold for a moment.

Len knocked at the front door. JB went to open it.

"I swear to God, JB, I've had more dealings with the police lately than a Times Square hustler. You and your meddling in other peoples stuff have made me the sweetheart of the Twenty-sixth precinct, and since I'm not a uniform queen it is a mighty uncomfortable position to be in."

JB spoke to Len's back as he went past him and headed for the kitchen table. "You report a dead person you're going to talk to the cops. It's kinda expected."

Sitting at the table Len continued grousing. "Well, it's become a very hard pill to swallow. All those questions. And they aren't very nice about wanting answers."

"Better than it being an suppository. Where's Sam?"

"He stayed with the police to harangue them until they get a ballistics match with the gun we found to the bullet out in Yonkers. He wants to make sure that Nicholas is released as quickly as possible."

"So the police accepted that the man we found dead was a sniper killer?"

"Regular citizens don't usually have rifles with scopes in their luggage. They're investigating it."

"Good. And Sam will work hard to get Nicholas out of jail, I'm sure."

"So, what did you find in the gym locker?"

"Oh." JB stood and went back to the door. He grabbed his backpack from the hook and returned to the table. "This." He pulled out the file folder and laid it down. "I think it's Dick's personal papers. It could give us a clue or two."

"To what? He's dead. Case closed, right?"

"Not necessarily. We still don't know why he killed Rosalie Stymington."

"Because he was hired to. That seems pretty clear."

"But who hired him, Len? Was it Nicholas? Or somebody else? And why Rosalie? She seems pretty innocent in all this. It isn't like she's a mobster or something. Why put out a hit on her? So, we're a long way from finishing up on this one."

"Lovely. Well, what's in the file?"

"I have no idea. I haven't looked yet."

"What's keeping you then?"

The kettle started to whistle. JB got up. "That, for one. Do you want tea?"

"Good God, we're stuck in the middle of one of those cozy old English mysteries. When does Lady Pennington admit to killing Lord Who's It, Miss Christie?" He reached for the folder and opened the flap to begin rifling through the compartments.

"Well, Lord Who's It, what are you finding?" JB said as he sat across from Len.

Len grabbed all the papers in one compartment. "Here, you look at those.", as he continued going through the file.

JB started separating the pieces of paper he'd been handed. He found receipts—it would appear even hired killers had to report business expenses—and then came across two passports. In two different names. One for Dick Rensler. Another for David Regis. Inside the passports were New York driver's licenses and social security cards for the same two people. Both pictures on the licenses were of the dead man. So he'd worked under assumed names. It looked like he had something in common with Nicholas, although the reasons for the identity switches were completely different.

The rest of the papers were of little interest— more miscellaneous items, gas receipts, store coupons, that sort of thing. Until he came across a checkbook. Much more interesting, JB was thinking. The register showed a balance of over two thousand dollars. Not exactly chump change, but not as much as JB would have expected him to have for killing someone. "Is there another bank book in there, Len? For a savings account maybe?"

Len looked up from the things he was looking at. "Yeah, there is." He fingered the divisions in the file, found the right one, and handed over the book. Then he went back to looking at what he had in his hands.

JB opened the savings book and went down the list of deposits and withdrawals. Most were for small amounts, fifty dollars here, seventy-five there. Then a deposit of sixty-thousand dollars the day after Rosalie Stymington was killed. That would be the payoff. If they could find out where that money had come from they might have the name of the person who hired the killer. "Look at this, Len. We'll have to give this bankbook to Sam, so he can hand it over to the police. They can trace the deposit."

"But that helps the police not us. And they aren't good about sharing."

"We have no choice. Unless you know how we can trace it ourselves."

"Nothing comes to mind. Maybe if we come at it from a different angle. Did you see these?"

"What?"

"Photos. Here's one of Dick and Nicholas. From the looks of them it was when they were in the Army." Len handed it to JB.

It was a duplicate of the one he had seen at Sam's. On the Nicholas shrine. "The two of them were friends in the service. I've seen this before. It's what makes this all so weird. And suspicious. Nicholas knew the man who killed his wife. It doesn't bode well for him."

"They also shared a girl." Len handed over another picture. It was a distance shot of an Asian woman on stage in a nightclub. She was standing, picked out by a spotlight, at a microphone, apparently singing with a three piece band. Guitar, bass, and drums. It was the costumes that were a shocker. She and the band members had on cowboy style outfits that would cause both Roy Rogers and Dale Evans intense envy. They were in colorful satins with fringe and spangles and cowboy hats. The woman brazenly shone and sparkled in the light of the spot, her ten gallon hat tipped back to show her face. An Asian country western singer in a foreign nightclub? If JB had to guess, located in Vietnam. Above the band hung a banner that read HAPPY CLUB etched in glitter. On the back of the photo was written "Song" and the year. Nineteen-seventy-three. Yep, that would make it Vietnam. Maybe Saigon? Lots of men took their R&R there during the conflict.

Len said, "There's a picture of the two of them with the girl too. So they both must have known her. Dick looks to have been really hooked. There are at least six or seven pictures of the girl here." He held them up spread like a magician doing a card trick. "All marked "Song" on the back. That must be her name."

"Probably. But it brings us no closer to finding out who hired Dick to kill Rosalie."

Len slipped the photos back into their envelope, then put the envelope back into the file. "Well, we're not going to find out anything more today." He checked his watch. "And I have to get to work. Broadway curtains wait for no man."

CHAPTER 13

The phone rang at JB's apartment at eleven the next morning. After Len had left the night before JB had worked on his novel until three so had slept in. He was shocked awake by the ringing. To keep it from doing it again he picked up. "Hello."

"Oh, did I wake you, JB? Sorry. Its Sam. I'm here with Nicholas."

JB wiped at his eyes. "Where? And not to mention how?"

"At my apartment. He's here with me. Once the police did the ballistics test on the weapon we found at the "Y" Nickola was in the clear. They couldn't hold him for more than forty-eight hours without charging him anyway. And once the gun matched to the bullet that killed Rosalie they had no cause. They had to release him."

"Well, that's good news."

"What I'm calling about is we have a plan. My lawyer has advised me there are bound to be some repercussions from Nicholas showing up after being gone these past seven years. He's suggested we take a deposition about where he was during that time."

"Isn't Nicholas still sketchy on that? His memory hasn't come completely back has it?"

"No, of course not. But George...that's my lawyer... has recommended a hypno-therapist who thinks he can break open some of the memories locked inside Nicholas' brain. We're having a session this afternoon. But we need someone to witness the deposition. Are you interested? We're meeting at one here at my apartment."

"Can I bring Len?"

"Of course. Two witnesses are better than one."

"Then we'll be there."

Len got out of the cab first. Then turned back to pay the driver. "JB, I swear on a junebug, I don't know why I keep letting you rope me into these things. Why do I always go along with your little lost boy causes?"

JB climbed out of the cab and headed for the door. "You're an annoying, whiney, narcissistic, diva."

"That was a rhetorical question, JB."

"What question?"

The doorman was missing—out on an errand or a break or something—so JB picked up the intercom phone and dialed Sam's apartment.

"Ha, ha. Very droll." Len came up beside JB.

The door buzzed and JB pulled it open.

"By the way, we're only supposed to be witnesses today, which means we sit back and watch."

"Life as theater. One more form of show business in the larger scheme of things. Thank you Mr. Shakespeare. That must be why I get mixed up in your shenanigans, JB. It's never boring."

Sam answered their knock almost immediantly. "Ah, you made it," he said. He ushered them in. "I had deli sent up. Help yourself." Then he introduced them to the assembled group. His lawyer, a stenographer to record the deposition on her portable stenotype machine, and the hypnotherapist, Dr. Melvin Windbush.

Windbush was middle-aged, with a Van Dyke beard, rimless glasses, and a black turtleneck. Missing was the feathered turban. Small to the point of tiny he might have been an escapee from a circus sideshow. JB had to bend to shake his hand.

JB whispered to Len, "Where did he come up with this one? From a Vegas showroom?"

Len grinned. "Like I said, JB. Show business. I love it. This should be fun."

"If it wasn't so serious. Nicholas has some big explaining to do, and if hypnosis can drag it out of him then I'm all for it. Its only a suto-science you know? The police have occasionally used it to get details from crime scene witnesses, so it might work here. I'm not holding my breath though."

The "doctor"—and JB used that term loosely, because he wasn't sure what accredited school would issue a degree in swami—had Nicholas sitting in a chair and was in the process of putting him in a trance state. He spoke to him in a soft voice taking Nicholas down flights of stairs, riding elevators to basement levels, and soothingly picturing green meadows. With rainbows and unicorns JB suspected. Nicholas was slumped in the chair with his eyes closed and seemed to be reacting to the suggestions the doctor was giving him. A compliant subject.

"So when does he start clucking like a chicken?" JB whispered to Len.

Windbush stood and spoke to the assembled group sitting in a semi-circle facing Nicholas. "He's gone under quite nicely. Now I'll have to do some regressions to take him back to the events you are asking about. The part of the brain that deals with memory is called the hippocampus..."

JB instantly pictured Hippopotami in letter sweaters carrying books to college classes. He grinned.

Len leaned over," What's with you?"

"I just think its funny. Amazing what a little flim and flam and some technical jargon will accomplish. No?"

"Well, wipe your chin. You've got a little bit of evil showing."

JB automatically put his hand to his chin.

Len smirked, then turned back to watch the doctor.

Doctor Windbush continued. "...and in Nicholas' case there is some bruising to that area. This is preventing him full access to his past. Regressing him through hypnosis will open some of the doors, but not all of them. There will still be areas that I'll be unable to get to. Some events can be so traumatic he won't be able to look at them yet."

JB knew what that was about. It was called a

disclaimer. If it didn't work then doctor had a way out, and still got paid for his time.

Doctor Windbush went back to sit next to Nicholas. JB went to the buffet to make himself a ham and cheese sandwich.

"Now, Nicholas, I want you to imagine that you are on a yacht and its sailing toward the horizon. The closer you get the further back you will be able to remember. Do you understand? Each foot the boat sails takes you back a year. Now it's Nineteen-eight-five, now eighty-three. Now its Nineteen-eighty. Are you there?" Nicholas nodded. "You have just gone out on a small rowboat for some fishing on the Hudson River. Do you see it?"

Nicholas answered, "Yes."

"Your line is in the water. Do you have any fish?"

"Can we get on with this, doctor?" Sam was impatient. JB was still doubting it would even work.

"Very well? Nicholas, please tell us what happened on that day in Nineteen-eighty? Can you tell us what happened to you?"

Nicholas seemed to sit straighter. His face screwed up in thought and he began to speak. "There was a rainstorm."

Sam said, "That's right. There was. A sudden storm came up that affected the whole area that day."

Nicholas kept talking, "I lost control of the boat. I was at the mercy of the churning water. The rough motion threw me down to the bottom of the boat. I hit my head." He stopped a moment. "I don't remember anything more until I woke up."

Hot damn, JB thought. Forget the chicken jokes. Could this really work? Have previously closed circuits started to reconnect inside Nicholas' pickled brain?

Nicholas stopped then. The doctor prompted him to pick up his story from when he finally woke from his accident.

"I was lying next to the overturned boat on a beach near Hastings On Hudson."

Sam specified the location. "That's about thirty miles up from Yonkers. The boat must have drifted."

Nicholas went on. "I didn't know who I was. I found some money in my pocket so I walked to the train station. I got on the first train that left. I didn't know where I was going. I meant to go home, but the train took me to Manhattan. I wandered around trying to figure out who I was."

"This is where the amnesia began?" the doctor said. Well, duh, JB was thinking. But he was now sitting back in the semi-circle listening intently. This was actually going to help.

Nicholas continued talking.

"First I was at Penn Station. Then I was at Grand Central. Its all fuzzy. Confused. I walked past Macy's. Then I was on Fifth Avenue. Why was I in the city? I kept walking. My head hurt and I couldn't figure out who I was or anything. It started to get dark. I was getting scared. And hungry. So I ate. A slice at a pizza place. I started walking again. Still on Fifth. At Thirteenth Street I stopped. In front of this club. There was a banner over the door. *'Too Much Ain't Enough'* it said. It was funny. And there was this huge iguana peeking from over the roof."

"Iguana?" What kind of sound does an iguana make? JB asked himself. "He's making this up, right? An Iguana? In Manhattan?"

Len said, "No, he isn't. I know the place. They have a fifty foot blue fiberglass iguana on their roof. It's the Lone Star Cafe. They feature country western singers."

Nicholas spoke again. "Kinky. Kinky Friedman

and his Jew Boys were playing. I knew about them. So I went in and sat down." He stopped for a moment. Then he said, "That's when I met Phan. He was there too. We got along so good. He loved the music. I did too. I'd listened to country when I was in Nam. Song was in a band. Phan reminded me of her. It was the first thing I remembered that day."

Len said to JB, "That's the person in the pictures we found."

JB nodded. "I know. Look at all this. Overturned buckets. Worms everywhere. Ask him about her, doctor."

"Nicholas, who was Song?"

Nicholas smiled. "A girl. She was beautiful. She was my sweetheart. I met her in Saigon. She was a singer. A hostess at The Happy Club." He sighed. "I loved her." He quieted, sitting, letting the pictures of the girl pass over his mind.

Sam said, "I've never heard of her. He loved someone other than Rosalie? Some girl in Vietnam? I had no idea."

"What happened to her?" JB asked. The doctor repeated the question.

"Killed. A bomb at the club. A Cong bomb went off. My leg was hurt then. It got me sent home." A tear ran from Nicholas' eye.

JB said, "You and your friend both knew this girl. You and Dick?"

Nicholas' entire demeanor changed in that instant. The look of panic he had exhibited at the house in Yonkers was back. His legs pulled up. He held out an arm and moaned, "Noooo."

Sam was standing. "What's up? What's wrong with him?"

The doctor said, "This sometimes happens. A word will trigger some other memory. Something stronger than what the subject is currently looking at. He'll be overwhelmed by this other event."

"What did I say?" JB looked at Len.

"You mentioned Dick."

Nicholas moaned again.

"That's it then. The name brings up something bad for him."

Doctor Windbush spoke to Sam. "Should we explore this, Mr. Bonanno?"

"Yes, I suppose so. We need to know."

The doctor spent some time soothing Nicholas' emotions. Calming him down so he could look at the event in a more detached way. Without the turmoil he was currently showing. Then he asked him where he was.

"The house. Hudson River House. In Yonkers."

"When is this?"

"Last week. Only last week. I was sent a newspaper article that said Rosalie was going to declare her husband dead. I didn't go to my appointment. Instead, I went to see her."

"Who sent the article?"

"I don't know. It was in the mail right before I left the studio. But the envelope was blank, with no return address. No stamp even."

That meant whoever delivered it did so by hand, JB realized. "So you went up to Yonkers?"

"Right. I knew the house and went right to it. When I rang the bell Rosalie came to the door. She was surprised to see me, but she invited me in..."

Sam spoke to the secretary. "Are you getting all of this?"

Nicholas' voice was choked. He continued in a rush, as if to rid himself of the horror of what had happened. "We talked. It didn't go well. It was bad. She was so angry with me. And frightened. She backed away from me. Afraid. She ran up the stairs. I followed. She couldn't get her door open so she backed out onto the widow's walk. She kept telling me I wasn't supposed to be there. I tried to explain. Then I heard the shot. A rifle. I knew that sound. I'd heard it before. Too many times. In Nam. Rosalie fell to the floor. Dead. The blood was spreading out around her head. Scared. I got scared. I backed away. I stumbled down the stairs and out the front door. I looked around. For where the shot had come from. Next door there was a man with a gun slung on his shoulder. Climbing down from a tree. He had to be the man who shot Rosalie. I chased him. When I got to him I grabbed at his shoulder and turned him to face me. It was Dick. I hadn't seen him for...for years. Since we left Saigon. He raised his rifle and hit me on the forehead with the butt of it. I went to the ground..."

"Then what happened?"

"I woke up. In an alley. In Greenwich Village."

JB sat back. "And that was his second case of amnesia. He was found the next morning not knowing who he was again."

CHAPTER 14

The hypnosis session over the doctor gathered his supplies and prepared to leave. JB went to him and asked, "He's going to remember all of this, right?"

"And possibly more. Often the memory once opened will pour out more information than the session had previously unearthed."

"Thank you. It was most interesting. I must admit I had some doubts, but you proved me wrong."

"I'm happy that it went so well. He was a most willing subject."

Sam stepped up and handed over a check. The doctor stuck it inside his coat, said goodbye, and left.

"Well, that was remarkable wasn't it, JB? Now we know for sure that Nickola didn't shoot Rosalie. We have his own eyewitness account."

"Actually there is other proof if we could get to it."

"What's that?" Sam and JB walked back into the living room.

"We found a bankbook that showed a large deposit into Dick's savings account the day after the killing. If we knew who it was from we would know who hired Dick. Unfortunately, I have no idea how we could trace it."

"JB, how do you think I pay for this Park Avenue apartment? I work as an executive at Banker's Trust. I can trace the deposit for you."

"Really? That's great. I was thinking we would have to turn it over to the cops to get any kind of trace on it."

"The less police involvement the better. I just got Nickola out of their clutches. I won't let him go back."

"I don't think I'm supposed to hear this." George the lawyer said. "Not if it makes me guilty of aiding and abetting. Sam, I'm going now. We'll have the transcript for you in a day or two."

"Great. Thanks for arranging this." Sam saw George and his secretary to the door, then returned to the living room.

"Now, where is Nickola? The poor boy must be whirling with all that's come out today."

"He went to the other room. Through there."

Len pointed to a hallway, then continued putting together the sandwich he was building at the buffet. Sam followed Len's finger.

Len took a bite from his sandwich and chewed for a moment. "You know, JB, I think I understand why you've gotten so involved with this boy. Hell, it looks like most everyone around him gets sucked in too. He's a Nora Needy. It's as if he's not able to take care of himself in the big bad world. He's like a waif out of a Dicken's novel."

"Len, he's thirty-five. With a successful interior design business. But, you're right. That juvenescent aspect about him is, I think, how he gets by. How he steers his way through the world. Some people use charm, some have been known to manipulate their way around. His callow youth act is what makes his life livable."

Sam was coming back to the living room. "Come along, Nickola, be hospitable. JB and Len are both still here. We should be nice to them." Said to Nicholas with a certain tone of indulgence it was a perfect example of what JB and Len had just been discussing.

Nicholas followed his uncle into the room and apologized for leaving. "I was on the phone. I just called Phan. I've asked him to come by the apartment later. We need to talk."

"We do too, Nicholas." JB beckoned him to sit on the couch. "What you said during hypnosis has brought up some more questions. Do you feel up to answering them?"

"Sure. I guess so."

"Good. Do you remember everything you said while you were under?"

"Most of it. What do you what to know?"

"I wanted to ask you about this Dick person. Where you knew him from? What sort of relationship did you have?"

"In the Army. I met him in bootcamp. That's all. We became friends and hung out together." Nicholas said this quickly, dismissively, almost defensive in its tone. He clearly wasn't comfortable with the subject.

JB thought back to the first day he had met Nicholas. When he was still Aric. Standing on a street in the Village wondering if he was gay. Hadn't he mentioned an event in a barracks shower? With another man? Who was blond and a friend? Was there something sexual between Nicholas and Dick? But now denied? Buried in some dark memory bank?

"Both of us were from around the same area," Nicholas was saying. "We were friends. That's all. Until we were sent to Nam. Then we were split. He went onto special training. Secret cloak and dagger stuff. He said he couldn't talk about it. I was stationed in Saigon. We met up a few times when we both were on leave over there."

Okay, JB was thinking. This is almost too much information. Trying to explain hook ups as just old fashioned male bonding. How hetero could you get? The "God, was I drunk last night..." defense.

"I never saw him again after I was sent back here to the world. It's been years. And then to have him show up in Yonkers. That was so weird."

"Very. You're sure that you hadn't seen him until that day in Yonkers."

Angrily he said, "JB, I can't be sure of anything. I don't even know if I can trust what I'm telling you now is fact or not. It's all just a big jumble of confusion inside here." He put his hands to his head. "Bits and pieces. Stray facts that keep floating to the surface. I'm pretty sure I hadn't seen Dick for years. Not until last week in Yonkers. Why was that, JB?" he pleaded.

"That's what we're trying to find out, Nicholas.

You said you two would meet up for R&R? Where was that?"

"In Saigon. We'd get a hotel room, away from base. We'd do the town together."

"At The Happy Club."

"Yeah. But how did you know about that?"

JB pulled out the picture of the girl with the band. "This was among Dick's things. It says 'Song' on the back. You mentioned her and the club under hypnosis."

Sam interjected, "You said you loved her, Nickola. You never told me about this before. I knew nothing about her."

"She was dead, Uncle. And in the past."

"Yet both you and Dick knew her, right? He had kept several pictures of her."

"I was young, JB. Away from home. She was a bar girl and I thought I was in love with her. So did Dick. We were rivals for her. It was kid's stuff."

"Maybe Dick thought it was more? It's a lot of year's later and he was still carrying pictures of her in his things."

"I can't say. It all gets fuzzy again."

"Okay. Then I have another question. That night you met Phan. At the Lone Star Cafe. How did you become Peter Sterling? Where did you get the name?"

Nicholas was quiet. Trying to pull information from the fog covered landscape that still functioned as his memory. "I did meet Phan that night. At that bar. We hit it off right away. I liked him. He was familiar somehow. I felt I already knew him. When I told him I couldn't remember my name we joked about it. Behind the bar was a bottle on a stand. Sterling Silver Vodka. We decided it was as good as any other name. He felt my crotch. He called me Peter."

"And that didn't make you uncomfortable? If you

were heterosexual wouldn't a gay.come on make you uncomfortable?

"It didn't though. He was so familier, like I said. I just felt okay about it. I don't know why.

At this point Sam, clearly not happy with what his nephew was admitting too, stood and began to clear the buffet. Busying himself in the kitchen, out of earshot.

Len leaned over to JB, "And a new person was created out some liquor merchandising and a groin grope. It's like Pygmalion with homo-erotic sex."

"Why not make it gayer than it already is, Len? I swear every time you open your mouth a tiara falls out."

Len sat back. "I'll remember you said that when you're old and begging for your heart medication, JB. Just wait."

Nicholas wasn't paying attention to them. He went on, "Then Phan and I moved in together. Right away. And we lived together for years. Like a married couple. But I have to tell him now. That's why I asked him to come over later tonight."

"To tell him what, Nicholas."

"That we can't live together any more. I have to break it off with him."

"That might not go over so well."

"I know. He is so unpredictable. But I still have to do it. It doesn't feel right being with him now. I'm going to stay here with Uncle. At least until I know more about myself. Its all such a mire right now. JB, would you stay while I talk with Phan."

"Oh, so you want witnesses."

"Sort of. He might not go crazy if there are people here."

"I will. But only because I'm curious.

Phan arrived just as Len was leaving the apartment for the theatre. He opened Sam's door to leave as Phan stepped up to knock.

Phan was wearing a Western style suit with a solid blue tie, his hair pulled back in a tail so he looked like a businessman attending a meeting. The only thing missing was the briefcase. He and Len hadn't met so they exchanged trivial pleasantries as Len finished putting on his coat. Nicholas and JB stood in the living room waiting for Phan to join them.

Nicholas, feeling anxious, wasn't looking forward to the sticky confrontation to come. JB was sitting back on the couch, in the position of fly and maybe bodyguard, depending on Phan's reaction to the news. Sam had still simply absented himself, not comfortable with the entire situation. He was old school Italian and still in shock that his nephew might have exhibited such a tendency to begin with. By distancing himself he could pretend it didn't exist. The Ostrich gambit.

"Phan, sit. Please."

He shook his head. "Say what you have to say, Peter. Or should it be Nicholas? Who are you?"

"Phan, that is the very reason I asked you to come here today. We have to decide what to do about this situation we're in."

"What situation? You maybe don't love me? Is that it? You don't want to be with me? After all we have been to each other. After all that we have built together."

"I'm afraid that is it exactly, Phan. I don't know what to do. You see I really don't remember all that you're referring to. I don't remember our past together. In my mind there is nothing to build on."

Now Phan sat. Heavily. On an ottoman nearby. His hands went to his face. JB leaned forward, expecting copious tears and banshee like wailing.

It didn't happen. Phan looked up at Nicholas. His face was set. A vein along his jaw throbbed. In a voice hard with decision, he said, "I tell you now, this...will...not...happen. We will not lose what we have. You won't leave me."

"Phan, you have to understand. I can't..."

He held out his hand like Diana Ross singing *Stop In The Name Of Love*. "Enough. Neither I, or my family, will accept this. You and I are partners. That is fact. It cannot be changed."

"You mean the design business? Well, I have some money. I'll buy you out, Phan. At a fair price, of course. That will sever that connection. And then we can go our own ways."

"You think it is that easy? You have no idea."

"Well, we'll have to go over the books, of course. Inventory the assets..."

"I said...That. Will. Not. Happen!" Phan was screaming now. The words slashed at the air, cutting Nicholas off. Shocking him into silence.

Phan turned on a heel and stomped to the door. He turned back. "You will be dead and gone before our story is over. You can not be done with me. The Tok cabal will not permit it."

He left, slamming the door behind him. Nicholas stood shock still where he was, a look of astonishment on his face.

"That was interesting?" JB said.

Nicholas turned on him. "Interesting? That was crazy. Insane and threatening. Downright scary. A hell of a lot more than just 'interesting'. The man's a lunatic, JB. He said I was going to die."

"Yeah, that did seem a bit over the top. Even for Phan. What I wonder about is the use of the word 'cabal'? Where did that come from?"

"He threatened me, and your looking at semantics? Now who's crazy?" Nicholas went to the bar and poured himself two fingers of Scotch. He tossed them back.

"What I mean, Nicholas, is Phan seemed more worried with what his family would think than what personal feelings it might concern. What does his family have to do with your business or his life? Do you remember them being involved in the design firm at all? And who would make up Phan's family?"

"He's Asian. They tend to have close ties with their families, don't they?"

"I suppose. It's been said they're always working for the next generation. For those that come next. But Phan is a gay man. No marriage. No children. There won't be a next generation. Let's see, he said he had a sister. But she's dead. And there's a brother. Is there a mother or a father?"

"I do remember one thing. There was a large gathering we went too once. A Sunday spent with a lot of people. Lots of food. A sort of picnic in someone's backyard."

"That could be the cabal he was talking about? We'll have to go by the interior design store tomorrow, Nicholas. Hopefully Phan will be calmer then. We can ask him about it then. We might get a reasonable answer out of him."

"Reasonable to that mad queen isn't the same as reasonable to you and me."

"Well, you probably define mad queen differently than I do. You're thinking more Desdemona than Rip Taylor aren't you?"

CHAPTER 15

Len knocked on JB's door with bowl in hand. JB opened and Len said, "Food, sir?"

JB smiled. "Consider yourself..." Matching Len's *Oliver* reference. "...invited in." He held out his hand, then walked to the kitchen. "What's with the bowl?"

Len closed the door and followed, "Fruit Loops.

I thought we could have breakfast together."

"Forgot to buy milk again, right?"

"I could have had my cereal European style. I have orange juice upstairs. Then I remembered you always keep a quart of milk in your icebox. Anyway, I wanted to show you this." He laid a magazine on the table in front of JB and went over to the refrigerator. "Look who's the cover boy this month."

JB leaned in. It was a new copy of *Mercenary Monthly: A Magazine for Hired Warriors*. A small picture of Dick on the bottom right was captioned: "We profile this month's Soldier of Fortune."

"Dick was definitely a hired killer then. He even publicized himself as one."

"Apparently. I didn't even know they advertised until I found that at the magazine stand last night."

"Where else would you find a war monger for hire? Do they have agents, like actors?"

"Maybe. But whom would kill whom?"

JB opened the magazine to the article and read. "Let's see...our boy was last in Pakistan. As a mujahedeen. Guerrilla fighter. Also in Afghanistan. Before that it was Iran, and Nicaragua. That's Iran-Contra stuff. I read congress is looking into all that. Our Dick was a busy boy. All the way back to Cambodia in the seventies. He was certainly experienced, wasn't he?"

"And, according to the article, available for..." Len held up two fingers and wiggled them. "... 'private assignments'. Like killing for hire."

"They say that?"

"Not outright. But they hint broadly. And check this out..." He reached over and flipped the pages to the back of the magazine. "...they have want ads. Just like *The Advocate*. SWM looking for same with 'killer' aim. No queens, fattys, or drags. Light bondage okay. Look. It's even categorized. 'For Hire' and 'Looking To Hire'. Its pretty blatant." He ate a spoonful of cereal.

"So, whoever hired Dick could have found him here easily."

"Right."

"It makes it harder for us to find out who did hire him then. I'm expecting Sam to call. He was tracing the deposit to Dick's account."

"By the way, what happened after I left last night?"

JB told Len how Phan had reacted to Nicholas' desire to end their relationship. "It was like a Pan-American Albee play. *Who's Afraid of Virginia Quang.* Phan was raving. And not in a good way."

"Isn't that the usual with him? That's what you said. Drama queen par-excellance."

"But this was different. He went on about family. The 'family' wouldn't allow it. I just wonder what sort of ties there are with his family. Nicholas remembers there being gatherings of large groups of people. But Phan had only indicated a sister and a brother. And the sister was dead."

"Cousins. Aunts. Uncles. Various kith and kin?"

"I suppose."

Len finished his cereal. JB sipped his coffee. The phone rang. "Maybe that's Sam." JB got up to answer. It was. JB took notes while he talked then hung up.

"He said the sixty thousand came from a business account. From a restaurant called Luann's. It's in the Wall Street area. You feel like lunch?"

"I just had breakfast."

"Its not my fault your three hours behind everyone else. Come on. Let's check this out."

"Shouldn't you be saying 'the game's afoot' or

something? If ever a moment called for it this would be it."

"How about I say get your ass in gear and leave it at that?"

"It has nowhere near the poetry of Conan Doyle, but it will have to do. Let me get my coat."

The restaurant was a hole in the wall. And was named Lu Ahn's not Luann's. American-Chinese-Vietnamese food. Chop Suey. Fried Rice. Noodles. Not much bigger than an alley dumpster it had eight tables covered in flowered oil cloth and a mixed bag of mismatched chairs. A bottle of soy sauce was the only table decoration. The walls were covered in faded airline posters for flights to the Orient. JB and Len took a seat at a table in the corner.

Len picked at a dried piece of old something that was stuck to the cloth and looked around. "Has all the charm of a tuna trawler, doesn't it?"

"I wouldn't order the fish if I were you. Maybe something not so prone to going off."

"That wouldn't be my stomach, I can tell you."

An Asian man in a limp almost white shirt with rolled up sleeves and a food stained apron to his knees came to their table. "You order?" he said. He had a mean and pinched little face. Like a beetle behind thick black framed glasses. He held up a pad and a stub of pencil.

JB said, "Are you the owner of this place? Mr. Luahn"

"I Lu Ahn. You health department?".

"No. No, nothing like that."

"Okay. I own. What you want?"

"Please sit. I was wondering if I could ask you some questions."

He stayed standing. "What questions?" He was

acting like a whore being arraigned on a Monday morning. Beligerent and un co-operative.

"We have it on good authority that your little restaurant here made a deposit of sixty thousand dollars into the account of one Dick Rensler last week. We were wondering why that was? What was it in payment of?"

The man's eyes were suspicious. "You cop?"

"Not that either. I'm a writer."

"Ah. Reporter?" JB nodded. A white lie to grease the wheels. "Money for help. Mr. Dick get my people out of Vietnam. Money for doing so. Mr. Dick good man. Help many of my people escape to USA. Pay is for gratitude. Now what you want?"

"More explanation, please."

"I say no more. What you want to eat? Order now." He stabbed his pencil at his pad.

"Uh, all right, in that case, I'll have the lo main noodles."

"Okay. You?" He turned to Len.

"Hot and sour soup."

"Okay. You wait. I bring." Lu Ahn went to the back.

"He's about as charming as the decor."

"Do you really think this tiny place could made that much money? I don't. I'll bet he doesn't even make enough to pay his rent out of here."

"Yeah, with only eight tables he'd have to turn them every few seconds to make anything at all. What about the rest of his story?"

"A lie. Complete and total. Prevarication alley."

"Don't hold back, JB. Say what you think."

"Well, did you believe any of it? A hired killer and soldier of fortune, out of the goodness of his oversized and generous heart, helps a man and his family get out of a war-torn country and into the protection of the good ol' US of A. Attention Hollywood. Your next *Rambo* movie is here. Not in character with our man. At all." He shrugged. "Bullshit is what it was. Bullshit is what it remains. We both know what the money was for."

Mr. Ahn returned with their food. He laid it down in front of them and turned to leave.

JB said, "Excuse me, Mr. Ahn. Does the name Rosalie Stymington mean anything to you?"

His grim face changed to puzzlement. "Who? Never hear of. Eat. You like." He left them to their food.

"Now that might have been the truth. You know what I think? This was simply a front. A place to filter the money through for the real person. The one who actually hired Dick."

They began to eat. The food was not bad. Peasant cooking straight from the Vietnamese countryside.

JB ate with relish but with an eye to the activity going on around him. "Len, have you noticed that we're the only one's eating?"

He looked at his watch. "It is a bit early. It's barely lunchish."

"No, that's not it. I've been counting how many people come and go. And its been brisk. Since we started eating there's been at least ten men in and out of this place. They come in, go to the cashier, give her money, she gives them a plastic thingy, and then they leave again. What do you think it is?"

"They have a fabulous 'to go' menu and the pick up window is outside?"

"I'm wondering where they're all going." He looked back at the cashiers stand. "Wait a minute, there just might be a way to find the answer. Excuse me a minute."

JB got up and went over to the cashier. He tapped the shoulder of the man currently handing over his money. A twenty dollar bill from what JB could see. The cashier handed him a tile piece from a mah-jongg set. A white plastic tile with oriental characters embossed on it.

"Hello. Why aren't you at the design shop?" JB said.

He had recognized the pimply young intern he had met that day at Sterling and Phan. He was dressed in a suit and tie this time and was looking very stock broker-ish with glasses and a briefcase, but it was the same boy.

JB held out his hand. "Do you remember me? We met at the interior design firm of Sterling and Pha..."

The boy quickly said, "Yes, of course..." He took his hand and steered JB away from where they were standing. "What a surprise." He chuckled and slapped JB on the back, but he was looking back at the cashier lady, who was eyeing them suspiciously. "Good to see you." Then he said in a softer voice, "Where are you sitting?"

Confused, JB pointed to where Len was. "Over there."

He took JB's elbow and moved him to the table, then sat next to Len.

"Len this is..." JB looked at the young man. "I don't know your name."

"Steve. Steve Kominski." He turned to Len. "Nice to meet you."

"Likewise." Len looked over at JB. "Who is he?"

"He works as an intern with Phan. At the interior design firm."

"Somehow I don't think that's his only job."

"You could be right. What's up?"

Steve sighed. "I'm with NYPD Vice. I'm a cop. Undercover. You're in the middle of a sting." He surreptitiously showed them his badge.

"Well, well. Then what was that all about?" He jerked his thumb back at the cashiers stand.

"I couldn't let you say the name you were about

to. It could blow our operation."

"What? Sterling and Phan?"

The boy nodded.

"Wait a minute. Operation? Your running a sting on this place? They must have one hell of a bad health violation."

Len pushed his bowl of soup aside, then looked at the kid. "You don't look old enough to be out of middle school. And you're a cop? Isn't he adorable, JB. He looks just like a bar mitzvah boy."

The boy nodded. "I've heard it before. I'm almost thirty, but being young looking works in my favor for this sort of thing. No one ever suspects me."

JB asked, "What sort of sting is this? It's a pokey little cafe. How crooked can it be? Or are you allowed to answer that question?"

"I probably shouldn't, but you're here researching a book, right?"

Ah, ah. Then his being recognized the first time he'd met the boy had helped. Thank God for his readers, although he hated to admit they were diminishing as more and more entertainment options presented themselves these days. Those damn Walkman's were everywhere. VCR's proliferated. And now CD's were coming along. What was next? Something with computers he would bet.

"Hey, could you use my name as one of your sources for a book?", Steve asked.

And thank God for the very human desire for even the slightest touch of fame.

"Of course. Right on the acknowledgement page when I tell the story."

"Okay." He leaned forward conspiratorially. "The money I paid her gets me into the back of this place. It's an illegal gambling den. But you already knew that, didn't you?" JB wouldn't dare disabuse him of what he was thinking, so he simply nodded. "Well, we're getting ready to raid it."

"Today?"

"No, but in the next few weeks. We're still gathering evidence right now." He held up the tile the cashier had given him. "This is all part of the Vietnamese Mah-jongg Triad."

"Triads? Here?" JB had heard of them, but thought them more Japanese in origin, like the Ninja, who had a history of being paid assassins. He'd also heard that the New York City Chinatown area was rife with Tongs, which was a Chinese term. They were gangs of toughs that dabbled in drugs and such. And now the Vietnamese had Triads? Iniquity has many faces.

"Three Vietnamese families have banned together to run the vice in the area. The Ahn family is one of them. Along with the Han's and the Tok's. The Ahn's run this joint."

"You were working at Phan's studio. Is it involved too?"

He shook his head. "Phan is a part of the Tok family, but we don't think he's very involved. He's considered a black sheep. Or rather a pink sheep. His lifestyle has alienated him from his family. As far as we know there hasn't been any contact between them for quite a while. I was placed there to gather evidence, but didn't find anything that would tie him to his brother's association. We're going to bring the whole illegal triangle down." He checked his watch. "And to do that I'll have to get back to work." He stood. So did JB. "What do you think you're doing?" Steve said.

"You think after what you've told me I'm going to miss going in there with you? Into a gambling den?"

"But you can't. For one thing, you don't have a tile."

"Oh no?" He left Steve and went over to the cashier. He handed over a twenty dollar bill, winked at her, and was handed a tile. He held it up for Steve to see. As JB walked back to where they were standing Len picked up the check from the table. "I'll want my fortune cookie too." And he went to the cashier. He was back with his tile in under a minute.

"All right. But you two have to be careful. And once we're inside I don't know you."

Steve led them out of the restaurant and down a narrow alley beside the building. They walked past a couple of fishy smelling dumpsters with black garbage bags spilling over onto the ground. He stopped at a marred and scratched metal door with an eyehole, pushed on a button at the side, which set off a buzzer inside. A minute later the door made an unlatching sound. Steve pulled it open and went in. JB and Len followed.

Once inside, first Steve and then JB and Len handed over their tiles to a sumo sized man in a too tight pinstriped suit. He grunted at them while pointing them through another doorway. A plastic mirrored hallway with twinkle Christmas lights strung along the ceiling led them into the casino.

It was about five or six times the size of the little restaurant that served as its front. Done up in crimson washed satin wallpaper, gold trim, and a painted dragon chasing its tail around the walls, it was ample enough to hold two blackjack tables and a standing roulette wheel. A row of four slot machines stood at the side of the door. There were also tables for playing Baccarat, FanTan, and Poker against the back wall. A bar stood beyond the slots. Lined with stools it had a B-girl posed on every other one. There was lots of stockinged thigh and sloe eyed looks being exchanged with the few drinking customers. Through the layers of smoke that hung over the room JB counted at least sixty or seventy gamblers at the various tables. Very busy for so early in the day. Vice could always draw an eagar crowd. JB was thinking back to a few early mornings when he himself had left the after hours Anvil Club after a night of abandoned debauchery.

Steve disappered into the crowd. Len looking out over the room said, "I'll be at the blackjack table. If I'm not back in fifteen minutes...I'll be at the blackjack table." and headed off. JB went over to the bar, ordered a ginger ale, and looked around. One of the B-girls sauntered over and put her hand on his leg.

"Gee, honey, thanks for the offer, but I'm gay. The only thing I want to mount is a production of *Gypsy*. You understand?" She giggled and moved on to someone more interested.

JB picked up his drink and wandered the room checking out the various games. There was none of the excitement that Vegas would have encouraged here. The room was cloaked in a heavy even deadly seeming silence. There was grim concentration from both the dealers and the players. This was high stakes gaming and the participants were not in any mood for joking around. At the poker table there sat one or two Wall Street types that the area would have drawn in. Beside them sat some of the scarier Asian types JB had ever seen. The type wearing thousand dollar shiny silk suits, sunglasses that hid the eyes, and obdurate expressions that you knew could get you killed if you tried to fuck with them. The Wall Streeter's were, without a doubt, going to be the losers in these games. The sweat beading on their foreheads and upper lips attested to that. JB decided not to put any money on any of the games, his Kansas bred frugal nature thinking there were far better holes he could pour his money down. Eventually he found Len sitting at his blackjack table with a pile of chips in front of him. A very large pile of chips.

"How much have you got there, Len."

"I don't know. A couple of thousand." He gathered the chips and swept them into his pocket. "I'll find out when I cash in."

"Ill gotten gains do no one any good, Len."

Len was walking toward the cage. JB followed. "Thank you, Miss Patience Goodiegoodgoody. You may climb down from that high horse you're on. As a matter of fact I was thinking of taking this pile and donating it to one of the gay groups. There's a new one called ACT-UP. They could probably use some seed money. Don't you think?"

"That's very generous, Len. I'm impressed.

"It should white wash these funds quite nicely.

"Like Tom Sawyer meeting a new fence."

JB and Len cabbed back to their building from the Wall Street area. They were standing in the lobby, about to go to their respective apartments, when JB's door opened.

"What's this?" JB was startled. He'd locked his door before he left. He knew he had. Was it an intruder with lousy timing? Nicholas Bonanno stood in his doorway.

He definitely had to get his keys back from this guy. He was beginning to turn up as often as a fat tick on a slow dog, as one of Len's southern quips would have it. JB went into his own apartment with Len following.

"What's happened, Nicholas?"

"How do you know something happened?"

"This is just a social call?"

"Something's happened."

"Then you should have a seat and tell me. But first, why not give me back my keys? You don't really need them anymore, now do you?"

He held them out. "No, I suppose I don't. And you'd rather I called the next time I need to see you?"

"Very perceptive. Now what's up?"

"Remember you said that we should wait for Phan to cool down and then talk with him again? Yesterday. At Uncles?"

"Yes."

"I gave him until today. So, I went down to the studio to try to work out what we should do."

"About the business and that you don't want to stay with him anymore?"

"Right. That."

"And was he more receptive to it this time?"

"He wasn't there."

"Then just go back another time."

"No, you don't understand. Phan has gone. Completely. The studio was empty. All the furniture was gone. Everything. The place was vacant."

"He moved?"

"That's what it looks like. I managed to get into the building from the back and even the apartment upstairs is empty. It's a shell, JB. Phan has completely disappeared."

"You have to admit that is one dramatic gesture," Len chuckled. "I do love a good drama queen."

"And I've got to find him, JB. If nothing else there's a lot of money tied up in that business, and he's taken it all." Nicholas was sounding perturbed. "It makes no sense. To just vanish in the middle of the night like that. I would have been fair with him. He wouldn't have lost anything. I don't get it. What can we do, JB?"

"Well, first I would follow your own suggestion and find him. Now, how would we go about that?"

"I don't know, JB. That's why I came to you."

"I was asking myself the question, Nicholas."

"He often has conversations with himself," Len explained. "Its like good cop, demented cop inside that head."

JB had begun pacing, questioning himself. "He probably didn't go far since he managed it so quickly. That means he's probably still on the island of Manhattan. But to do it as fast as he did? He couldn't have packed it all by himself. So there had to be others involved. Who do you think that could be? His family? He did mention them yesterday. But Steve said he's on the outs with them. Or is he?"

"I see what you mean, Len," Nicholas said.

"Do you have the home number for your intern at the design firm?"

"Are you asking me?"

"Yes, Nicholas. Who else would I ask?" Len and Nicholas exchanged looks. "Do you have your book? His name is Steve." JB was sounding impatient.

"Yes. Okay. Phan gave it back to me. When we met him that first time. It's in my case. Just a second."

Nicholas checked and found the number. JB dialed. "Ringing...Rats, its his machine." He spoke into the phone. "Steve, this is Jeremy Bent. I had a question for you concerning Phan. Could you call me..." And he left his number. "We'll just have to wait until he calls back. Can I get you two something?"

"What are you going to ask Steve about?" Len asked.

"What? Oh, if Phan has another studio here in town. I thought that would be obvious? He has to have a second location. Or where does he keep all his decorating supplies? Fabrics, rugs, furniture. That stuff. I didn't see any place you could have stored anything there at the office. So there has to be another place where you kept it. Maybe you know where that was, Nicholas?"

He dug deep trying to think. His brain was still trying to dredge up the bits and pieces of his past. It had to be like a webwork maze in there. But this bit of information didn't seem to be one of them he could grab hold of. "I'm sorry, JB. But you must be right, there has to be some other place. I wish I could help you."

"Not to worry. Steve should know. But you know what, there is something I would like you to try and remember. Are you willing?"

"Sure. What do you want to do?"

"Something similar to what the hypnotist did yesterday. You seem to respond to questioning very well. It seems like a specific question will open up other details for you."

"He means you're like an onion, Nicholas. Peeling off layers like a stripper in the burly-cue. Should I hum *Night Train*, JB?"

"Thanks for the offer, Len. But it won't be necessary. Nicholas, if you would just sit back and relax, maybe we'll get some of those details out of you. Want to try?"

"Sure. If you think it will help."

"Okay. So close your eyes and let your mind wander." He sat back on the couch. JB waited a moment or two then asked, "I want you to think back to when you were in Vietnam. When you were stationed in Saigon."

"Okay."

"I'd like to know more about the day you were wounded. In the leg wasn't it?"

"That's right. There's a scar on my leg from the blast."

"The blast from the bomb that destroyed The Happy Club?"

He nodded.

"So was the club open for business when the bomb went off?"

He thought a second. "No. It was a Sunday. Early."

"So it was just you and your girl there? What was her name? Was it Song?"

"That's it."

"Where were you? Where in the club I mean?"

"We were upstairs. The family had living quarters up there."

"So were you in bed? That early on a Sunday morning."

"No. I don't think I was. But I was there...and it wasn't the blast itself that hurt us. It was the building collapsing around us. There was a beam that fell on the room."

"On you and Song."

"Yes...No...Wait. Dick was there too. It was the three of us, I think."

"So he was hurt too? Why was he there?"

"Perhaps a ménage?" Len said.

"Was that it, Nicholas? Were the three of you in bed together?"

"I don't know. But Dick wasn't wearing any clothes. He was naked. Why was that?"

"Like I said. A ménage. Kinky."

JB waved his hand at Len to hush him."What about you, Nicholas? Were you undressed too?"

His face screwed up in thought. "I don't think so. No. I was dressed. In uniform. But then why was Dick there? Like that? I don't get it?"

"What about Song?"

"She was killed. She was naked too. The MP's found her like that. She was crushed...under a beam that fell."

"Okay."

The phone rang. Startling everyone. Nicholas' eyes flew open. He sat forward. "What?"

"I'm sorry. I should have turned the bell off." JB stood and went to the phone.

"Gave me a heart attack." Len rubbed at his chest.

"Me too. Why was he asking me about that?"

"I have no idea. JB puts little random facts together and somehow comes out at the end with a story accompli. Its some sort of abstract thinking he does. It's quite remarkable to watch. Like a mouse in a maze finding the gorgonzola."

JB hung up the phone. "That was Steve. He didn't know of any other place that Phan had. But he did give me the address of Phan's family offices. The Tok Association. Nicholas, you said you remembered attending some sort of large gatherings. Was it with the Tok family?"

"I only remember one event. It wasn't very nice. Phan got into a huge argument with another man and we left in the middle of it. There weren't any others after that."

"When did that happen?"

"Right after we met. And I don't think he had any other contact with them after."

JB checked his watch. "Its still early. We should go to the Tok offices and see if they know anything. You want to come Len?"

"I don't think so. As puzzling as all this is I think I'd rather come in for the denouement at the end. Let me know when your ready, Monsieur Poiret."

CHAPTER 16

The Tok Association offices were on Pell Street right off of Mott in Chinatown. Formally a tourist gift shop the four story brick building was painted a cinnamon bar red with the step cut pagoda roof corners often used to decorate structures in that part of town attatched to the the second story. The open front had gold capped red paper streamers hung between lacquered circular columns. These held up a small wood scroll cut ornamental balcony.

The Tok Association's headquarters were upstairs through a hole cut at the side of the building. The bottom section was given over to a pachinko and mah-jongg parlor. Old men sat at rows of tables slamming pairs of tiles in the obsessive matching game as Nicholas and JB climbed the stairs.

Inside was a standard modern office with a receptionist right then speaking on the phone. She held up a finger to indicate she had seen them and to wait a moment. She finished her call, wrote a note on a pad, and looked up. "Good afternoon. How may I help you?"

"Yes. We wanted to see the boss. Is he available?"

"Mr. Lane Tok?"

"Is that the father or the brother of Phan Tok?"

"Oh, his brother. Is this in reference to Phan?"

"Yes. It seems he's gone missing. Perhaps Mr. Tok can help us find him."

She stood and asked them to wait while she tottered on stilitto heels to a polished mahogany double door and entered. A few minutes later she returned and indicated for them to go into the office.

Lane Tok stood as they entered. The office was done in a modern minimalist style. Large expanses of pale carpet with giant abstract paintings on the walls. A thick pane of glass on chrome sawhorses served as the desk. Lane was younger than Phan, maybe twenty, and much more dignified. Not a trace of the flamboyant Oriental facade Phan affected and wore regularly. Lane was wearing an expensive tailored suit, a brightly colored designer tie, and when he stepped out from behind the desk, a pair of black high top tennis shoes. Comfort over looks. Youth over conservative formality.

Where Phan still retained some of his accent Lane spoke with perfect English diction. The result of arriving as a younger child and assimilating to New York quicker than Phan, JB figured.

"Please have a seat." Lane indicated two clear Lucite chairs set in front of his desk. He returned back to his own chair and said, "My secretary told me you were looking for my brother Phan? Is that correct?"

"Yes. Mr. Bonanno here was the partner in Phan's interior design studio. Yesterday, when he went to see Phan, he discovered that the building that housed the studio was now empty and abandoned. Phan had taken everything and left with no forwarding address."

Lane had a malevolent look on his face. "I am aware of who Mr. Bonanno is. We've met before." Nicholas, for his part, looked surprised. "Are you aware that there is some animosity between Phan and his family? In fact, he has been banned from the family until he changes his ways. I have not spoken with my brother for several years."

Steve had said that Phan was on the outs with them because he was gay. "I'm sorry if I'm opening old wounds. But there is a great deal of money involved in the business they owned together. Phan has basically absconded with all the assets."

"I am not responsible for my brother's actions. That he might also be a thief does not surprise me. It is part and parcel with the life he has chosen to live."

An interesting conclusion, JB was thinking. Especially if Steve's vice squad investigation was correct. A pot calling another pot night time colors. Was he intimating that being gay and being a crook were one in the same? Talk about your obsolescent thinking.

Nicholas had been sitting quietly while Lane and JB talked. Now he spoke up. "I do remember you. You were the one that Phan had the argument with that day. At the picnic."

"True. And you were the person we were arguing about. Phan had flaunted his degenerate lifestyle too many times with our family. It was disgusting. Bringing you, his fancy man, to one of our events was intolerable. That day he had brought shame on our family one more time and I would not stand for it again."

JB interjected. "I take it that you don't approve of a gay lifestyle? That is a pity. Many would conclude that it's outdated and provincial thinking, especially here in Manhattan. Thievery, however, is still not approved of. Anywhere, that I know of. And straight people steal too."

Lane stood and spoke to them in a measured voice filled with the malice of his convictions. "Sir, the Vietnamese community does not approve of perverts or degenerates. We hold to a long tradition of marriage and respect for family. Phan would not follow his father's wishes and become a husband and father. He was therefore banned. It's simple."

"And stultifying. His father, and perhaps his brother too, would have been better off to learn something about acceptance."

"It was Phan's duty to accept what his family required of him. He chose to live the way he did. Father did the only thing he could in those circumstances. My father ran this family according to our custom. And prospered by it. That is up until two years ago. That's when Father became ill. A heart attack. It took everything from him. Now he sits downstairs and plays mah-jongg all day. I took over the Association when he got sick and I run it according to his dictates. This is what he decreed to be Phan's penalty for defying the family. It is therefore just."

"It is biased and judgmental. And quite reprehensible. Phan's life was his own. Following his instincts was very brave. Noble almost."

"Noble. Wallowing in the muck? I remember the queer boys when I was small. Back in Saigon. Flaunting themselves. Dressing as girls. As whores. Whistling after soldiers from their dirty bars. Giving sex to the GI's in back alleys..."

"Didn't your sister work in one of those bars? That's the impression I got from a photo I saw at Phan's. Need I mention people and glass houses?"

"What do you know about Song? She was a good, sweet person. Angelic. You have no idea what it was like back then. We did what we had to do to survive."

Nicholas started. "Your sister's name was Song?" he asked.

"That's right. Song Le Tok. She died. Now I think I have nothing more to say to you. You will both get out of my office."

They stood and left. In the lobby JB turned to Nicholas, "Well, that didn't accomplish much did it? I should have known better than to argue with a bigot. It never gets anything done, and only makes them more self righteous than they were before."

"Did you hear him, JB."

"What?"

"He said that his sister's name was Song. Was it a coinicidence? Or could it be the same one? The girl I knew?"

"How common is the name Song in Vietnam? Come on. I want to go downstairs."

"To the mah-jongg parlor? Why?"

"I want to talk to the father. I don't know if I believe that Phan and his father don't see each other. A son is a son, no matter what."

"But Lane said..."

"And who better to be a replacement daughter than a gay son? Come on."

JB took off. Nicholas, before he followed, went over to the secretary and spoke with her for a moment. Then he went after JB.

The parlor was an open space filled with flashing pachinko machines lined around the outer walls. The standing pinball mechanisms clicked and clattered as little steel balls were pushed up by players to run the nailed and spiked course of the gameboard. Lights blinked and bells rang as points were tallied on electronic counters attached to the machines. The center area of the parlor was filled with rows of tables where games of mah-jongg were played. The clacking of the game tiles as they were moved around their layouts aided and abetted the general buzz of the parlor. Ropes strung from corner to corner across and over the space displayed colorful banners and flags advertising God only knew what? The lettering was all in Vietnamese calligraphy. Standing electric fans in the corners, used to dissipate the cigarette smoke, kept the flags swaying back and forth in their mechanical breeze. A red painted caged cashiers booth over on the side sold the tokens used for the pinball machines, and if truth be known, for the patrons to gamble on the mah-jongg players games.

JB went to the booth and asked after Mr. Tok the elder. He was sitting at one of the back tables, alone, playing a solitaire game. The tiles were laid out in a traditional pattern and he was quickly matching like tiles and pulling them off to the side. He was grinning and speaking to himself, "I will beat you this time. I will. I will," he mumbled. As if the game itself were a living breathing opponent.

Mr. Tok was very old, with sparse white hair and wild long eyebrows over heavy sagging lidded eyes. In his eighties JB would have guessed. He must have had his three children very late in his life. With a younger second wife JB guessed. The Charlie Chaplin way of family making. "Excuse me, Mr. Tok."

He waved JB away. "Not now. Not now. I can win." Still engrossed in his game he continued matching tiles, clicking them together as he put them aside and chuckling to himself.

JB had read how addictive the game of mah-jongg could be, finding the match to each tile in the layout, although he could see no real strategy to the random placement of the tiles. To each his own, JB figured. He sat across from the old man.

"I was hoping we could talk for a moment, Mr. Tok."

The old fellow was scrutinizing his tiles, not finding any more matches. "What do you want then?" He sighed and began to shuffle the tiles for another game.

Nicholas had come up beside the table. JB asked him to keep watch. The father of a Triad organization leader would probably have bodyguards. Then he turned back to the old man. "I was wondering, sir, if I could speak with you about your son? Phan?"

"Phan. That scalawag." He snorted, still concentrating on the tiles in front of him. "What has he done now? Has he been up to more mischief? I will speak with him. And his brother Lane An too. The two of them are a handful. Perhaps they will be better in America. We are going soon."

That's when JB realized the sickness his son had referred to wasn't only a heart attack. Something else had taken the old man away from the day to day business of the Tok Association. Medically becoming known as Alzheimer's, the majority of people still called it simply senility or dementia. The elder Tok was lost somewhere in the past.

JB reached over and touched Mr. Tok's arm to get his attention. "No, sir, you've already arrived in America. Remember. You've been here for quite some time."

He waved his hand. "Yes. Yes, of course. The boys are in school, aren't they? Is that what the trouble is?"

Still somewhere in the past, but some years later at least.

The old man rambled on. "Phan is at Parsons, you know. Going to be an artist. Always at his studio. Painting. Making things. Chairs. Tables. He turned out to be a good boy. But so odd. He's flighty that boy. Different. But Lane is a joy. At high school now. Grade A student. I'm proud of my boys." He smiled and wiped a glob of spittle from his mouth.

JB tried to direct the conversation more to his current concern. "You should be proud, Mr. Tok. Uh, what if I wanted to see some of Phan's art work? Would that be possible? Where is the studio he works in? Maybe I could see it there."

"You might buy some of his art? That would be nice of you. His studio is close. On Henry Street..." and he rattled off the address as if it was fresh in his mind. For the old man lost in the past it probably was. He then went back to his game—searching the patterns on his tiles for matches.

Nicholas tapped JB on the shoulder and pointed. JB looked up and saw three heavy set, very determined, very mean looking men walking down the aisles between the players, aiming for their table. The old man's bodyguards? It had to be. So what to do? They didn't look as if they wanted to ask them out for a stroll in the garden. Exit was cut off from all sides. Going back wasn't an option since there were only rows of machines along the back wall and no door to use as egress. What was he to do? Go up?

And that is exactly what JB decided to do. He stood and said, "Thank you, Mr. Tok. You'll have to excuse me." Then he stepped from his chair to the top of the table the old man was playing on. He heard a yelp from him as JB's feet sent the old fellows mah-jongg tiles flying in all directions. Next JB took a giant leap of both body and faith and grabbed at the multiple ropes of flags strung across the room. Praying that they would hold his weight he swung himself off the table and like a circus trapeze artist he flew over the tops of the goons heads to land ass over teakettle on another players table.

Nicholas, meanwhile, had chosen a back and sidewards trajectory for his escape. This move was caused by his collision with the beefy hands of one of the guards pushing him down the aisle he was standing in. That push took him up against the row of pachinko machines along the side wall. He crashed into one of them, hard, which caused the glass cover on the machine to shatter. That sent the contents—what must have been a thousand little silver steel balls—to roll out over the floor in an ever widening wave. The guard who had pushed him was by then moving in for the kill, obviously planning to smack Nicholas around some. His raised balled fists were aimed for Nicholas' face until his feet were surrounded by the rolling steel balls on the floor. His feet hit those and he was suddenly in the air, arms flapping, flipping and slamming all two hundred and eighty some odd pounds of himself right onto the ground. Nicholas, quickly perceiving that his escape route had opened up, took off down the side aisle and aimed directly for the front of the shop, while the other bodyguards were occupied with getting their colleague back on his feet.

JB rolled off the table he'd landed on, apologized to the two gentlemen who's game he'd interrupted, and quickly caught up with Nicholas.

"Maybe we should leave?"

"Are you kidding? Maybe we should run our asses off," JB and Nicholas headed outside. The goons remained inside, abandoning their chase, seemingly concerned only with old Mr. Tok's safety.

Outside, while making their way toward the avenue, JB told Nicholas, "I got an old address for Phan. Maybe he's kept his studio in his old neighborhood for all these years."

"Did you ask the old man about his daughter? What did he say?"

"No, I didn't ask. I bearly got the information I did. I didn't want to confuse the old guy. He's not really here."

"I asked the secretary upstairs about how common the name Song is in Vietnam. She said it didn't come up much any more. It was very old-fashioned. Only the old people would have used it."

"Well, Mr. Tok was certainly that. I'd bet even his watch has liver spots. Come on, the address he gave me is close. We can walk."

CHAPTER 17

The address the old man had given them was a nineteen-twenties car garage converted now to other uses. The original green painted double doors with their paned windows along the top were still intact. A chipped enameled tin sign at the side still advised that to enter one should honk their horn. Nicholas stood on tiptoe and peered in one of the windows. "It's a warehouse, JB. Full of pallets with boxes on them."

"Who are they addressed to? Can you read them?"

"They're stenciled Sterling and Phan. Then there's Vietnamese writing. Like we saw at the mah-jongg parlor. They must be imports of some sort. But it means this is still Phan's place."

"Good." JB tried the handle of the entry door within the double doors. "Its locked. We need to get in there."

"There must be another entrance." Nicholas walked to the alley beside the building. "Here, JB." He disappeared down the alley. JB trailed after him.

Midway down was a canopied mullioned door with a stone urn filled with greenery on each side and a coconut mat between. Nicholas went to that door and tried the knob. "It's locked too." JB pushed the intercom and waited. No answer. He pushed again. Still no answer. They both looked up and down the alley.

"How are we going to get in, JB?"

JB spied further down the alley a four paned window at ground level. He headed for it. "Maybe this will work." It was made of a metal frame with the frosted wavy patterned glass often seen in bathrooms as shower walls. It was thick enough to offer some protection and sufficient to block any view of the inside. JB pushed on it. The window wouldn't budge.

Nicholas, who had continued to the far back end of the alley, came back. "There's a rear entrance, but its a steel pull down door with a padlock. Any more idea's?"

"We could come back another time. Or..." JB turned his back to the window, raised his foot, and with his heel kicked back as hard as he could at one of the panels. The glass cracked from the blow. Three more solid kicks and a small opening in the pane of glass was begun. A few more kicks pushed a couple of pieces of broken glass down into the now visible basement area of the studio. JB bent, wrapped his jacket around his hand, and punched at the cracked glass, which soon enlarged the hole. "...or, we can go in here right now." He reached in and unlatched the window. "One at a time I think." He stood and indicated that Nicholas should climb inside first. "And be quick. We don't want any stray cops to see us."

The five foot drop into the darkened basement was easy enough. JB and Nicholas were both inside in moments. The basement was dimmed and shadowy, filled with several work benches lined along the walls. They each held pieces of furniture in skeletal stages of completion. A chair on one, a settle on another.

"I remember something. Phan and I would find used designer furniture and restore it for resale to our customers. It was the bulk of our business," Nicholas whispered.

"This must be where the restoration work was done," JB whispered back. But he spoke to a blank space as Nicholas had gone off on a search of his own, disappearing into the dark of the basement, leaving JB alone. What he was looking for JB wasn't sure.

In the light from the broken window JB spotted an electrical box over one of the benches and went to it. He found the right switch and flipped it. A series of hanging florescent lights flickered and came on. That should make it easier to check out the workroom JB was standing in.

He could see several pieces of furniture down at the opposite end of the basement. A row of Mission style sofas, a gaggle of chairs, multiples of end and coffee tables. Furniture, from the looks of them, designed by Eames, Henry Miller, Frank Lloyd Wright, Stickley, Eileen Grey; all notable designers of the Arts and Crafts and mid-century style that Sterling and Phan seemed to favor.

JB went to check them out, assuming they were there waiting to be restored. But he found they were all in excellent condition for pieces designed as far back as the twenties and up to the fifties. The upholstery was fresh, the wood was satin shined. Already restored then? But there were so many pieces? He counted ten sofa's alone, and there were still more rows of tables and chairs.

He went back to the bench and looked at the settle being worked on there. It was a Stickley style couch of about Nineteen-twelve vintage. Nicholas had said they restored furniture, but on inspection, the wood in the piece he was looking at was new, as were the nails. It was beat up, gouged and scratched, but definitely new wood. There were no signs of the wear or use that would be expected on a piece of that age. The nails were old style with square heads, but unused. Old stock from an out of business hardware store perhaps?

He checked the shelf at the back of the bench. Varnish, steel wool, jars of various shapes of tacks. All of the usual supplies. However, there were also a few items not so usual. JB was beginning to suspect that all was not on the up and up. But he needed confirmation. Where was Nicholas? He looked around. The man was nowhere to be found. JB spotted a wall phone to the side of the bench. He went to it and dialed a familiar number.

"Hello, Len? I'm glad I caught you."

"Are you done sleuthing already? That was fast."

"Actually, I'm still right in the middle of it, but I had a question that only you can answer." Flattery could get him very far with Len.

"Really? What?"

"In that course on antiques you took at the New School did you study the art of fakery?"

"Where are you?"

"In the basement of Phan's studio. On Henry Street. It's an old garage that's now a furniture workroom. Nicholas said they restored furniture, but I'm not so sure that's what's going on here. Some of the stuff I found here is pretty odd."

"Like what?"

"Well, how about a jar marked French earth? What would you use that for?"

"Its also called rotten stone. It's powered volcanic ash. For faking things its used as an additive to varnish. To age a surface. To add a false patina."

"That's what I thought. What kind of prices are pieces by Stickley bringing now?"

"Stickley furniture? It's an up and coming category. Some pieces can bring upwards of four figures."

"How about an Eames chair?"

"Even more. A chair with ottoman will run you nearly two thousand new. Depending on condition you could get three or four for an original. What's this about?"

"I think Phan is running a counterfeit furniture workshop here. Making fake mid-century furniture to sell to his customers as the real thing. You remember saying you were white-washing that money you won?"

"Of course. Making ill-gotten gains clean again."

"That's what I believe Phan is doing for the Tok Triad. All that gambling and vice money has to be laundered somewhere. Selling forged furniture made in Vietnam to unsuspecting collectors would do exactly that."

JB heard Nicholas yelling to him from the upstairs area.

"JB, could you come up here. Right away."

"That's Nicholas calling, Len. I've got to go. I'll talk to you later..."

"JB, wait..."

He hung up.

Nicholas called again.

JB answered back, "Coming."

But not before he picked up a chisel from the work bench. Doing something similar to what Nicholas had done with his watch the night he was mugged, JB slipped it up the sleeve of his jacket. The elasticized cuff would hold it in place. Afternoon's spent watching reruns of old *Cisco Kid* and *Lone Ranger* TV episodes as a kid had taught JB to beware of ambushes. No way was he going to be bushwhacked, pardner. Who says television is an educational wasteland?

He slowly climbed the stairs one at a time until his head barely stuck above the ceiling boards. It was just high enough to allow him to see onto the next floor. He spotted Nicholas sitting a few feet ahead of him on a solid wood high backed chair with decorative cutouts showing above his head. A Frank Lloyd Wright design. At his chest was wrapped several turns of silver duct tape, holding him to the chair, preventing him his freedom. JB also felt a gun barrel stick itself against the back of his head.

"You come up now. Sit in other chair."

Phan Tok held the gun, which made him ad hoc director of this unfolding little drama. He pushed the cold metal against JB's head harder and said, "Come. Get up here."

JB took the rest of the steps with Phan beside him, the gun moving from his head to his back as he emerged fully onto the first floor, his arms held up cowboy style. He took the few extra steps to sit in another Lloyd Wright dining room chair next to Nicholas. Wright was a small man and designed all of his furniture for himself. If other people were taller, or bigger, it was considered their problem not his. The arrogance of genius. The size of the chair meant that JB's knees were up at his chest with the tall straight back standing several inches above his head.

"Is this chair another one of your fakes, Phan?"

"You guess about that, huh? It will be the death of you then."

Uh, oh. Threats. So soon? Bullying of this sort was never good in these sorts of situations. How was JB to handle this one? There wasn't much he could do, except bluff and keep it going for as long as possible to buy some time. Time to think of an out. Any out. As viable as any other option, he supposed.

Phan stuck the start of a roll of duct tape to JB's jacket and began winding it around his chest and the chair. Several layers later he brandished his gun at JB and said, "Hands behind, please."

Polite meanness was still just meanness. Like serving tea at an execution.

JB used another of his childhood TV lessons to hold out his hands in a particular way. He held them fist to fist instead of wrist to wrist. It was a trick Houdini the magician used in his escape act. Once his wrists held in that pose were wrapped in the tape JB could then open his hands and be loosely held in the slack the difference in position afforded. It was also a position that would afford him working room to untape himself.

Phan came to the front and stood facing his two captives, still pointing his gun at them. He was dressed all in black, from his turtleneck to his shoes. Grim looking, certainly meant to be intimidating. Even his manner was lacking the flamboyance that had characterized him up until then. He was actually acting kinda butch like, without the gestures and arm flapping he had indulged in before. Even his voice had a lower timber, and no lisping as he said, "You have meddled in affairs you shouldn't have. You both will pay for it."

JB jerked his head. "Point that in another direction, Phan. We're not going anywhere." He lowered the gun. "What's with the virile act anyway? I sort of miss the theatrics."

He tapped his chest. "This is real me. That other is phoney. Nobody take that person serious."

"So you could get away with your money laundering scheme without suspicion. Clever."

"Aren't we Asians all supposed to be wily? That's what you expect."

Nicholas asked, "What scheme, JB?"

"Phan is still a member of the Tok Triad, Nicholas. He takes dirty money they earn from, among other things, gambling and cleans it up for the association."

"How?"

"He makes fake antique furniture to sell to unsuspecting collectors. Isn't that right, Phan? Where's the factory anyway?" JB looked around at the pallets filling the warehouse. "This all had to come from somewhere."

"In Vietnam. Furniture made there. In our own factory. Then send it here. Not antique so it fly through customs. Then we age and prepare it here."

"You're right. You are wily. Illegal money spent in a foreign country then all the cleaned up profits made here."

"But you have to get in middle. Mess up whole deal."

"Gee, sorry about that, Phan. I'm so sorry I messed up your completely criminal operation here. How long do you think you're going to get away with this, Phan? You think the authorities won't catch on? That some customer won't complain when he finds out he's bought a fake?"

"It works okay until now. Will again." He held the gun in JB's face. "When you gone."

"How are you going to explain two dead bodies, Phan?"

"I manage. Have before. Will again. Whole family good at cleaning up bumps in business. In fact, I like doing it. Especially to him." He pointed at Nicholas.

"So much for love and fidelity between lovers. I suspected there was something more than the family business at stake here."

Phan snorted. "Love? You think I love him. I hate him. Always have."

"Yet you lived with him for seven years."

"Old saying. Keep friends close, enemies closer."

"I always thought that was bad advice. Makes for stomach ulcers and excess bile. Heartburn night after night is a real bitch."

"Saying old, maybe not so good."

"So Nicholas is your enemy? Is that why you stalked him and found him that night at the Lone Star?"

Nicholas shook his head, befuddled. "But why, Phan? What did I do to you?"

Phan turned on Nicholas. He got right up in his face and rumbled, "You shut up." The menace in his voice was palpable, every word dripped venom. "You take life from me. You kill my sister. You murder my Song."

"I...I did what? I don't understand...Song? That girl was your sister?"

Phan was now screaming. Spittle showered Nicholas's face. "In Vietnam. At Happy Club. Morning of bomb. You kill my sister. My own dear Song. Innocent girl thrown into wreckage of building to die."

"Phan, please, I couldn't have. I don't remember, but I couldn't"

Phan by then had completely lost it. Years of held in hate and rage came pouring out of him. The over the top queen had once more appeared. Calliope playing, chariot rolling, horses rearing. Drama on drama on drama. Phan's face was screwed into pure loathing. "I saw you, you bastard. I was behind bar. Hiding from blast. You throw Song down like trash. You kill her. I was there. I decide then to kill you myself. Your life for her life. But first I will destroy you. You take all from me. I have all from you. You pay for what you did."

Nicholas was beside himself. Pieces of that night were flooding his brain. Memories sat on for years came rushing at him. "No, Phan. It was Dick. He was there. He was the one who caused everything. It was him, Phan. Not me. Then the explosion. The beam falling. It killed her. Song was dead." He burst into tears. "I loved her, but she was dead. I didn't kill her. I didn't."

Phan screamed, "You did. I saw. You did." He raised his arm, the one holding the gun, and brought it down, smashing it against Nicholas' forehead. Blood poured from the jagged reopened wound still unhealed from his previous attack. Nicholas was out, his head lolling to one side. Phan stood over him, breathing heavily. Spent.

JB could feel the puzzle pieces finally dropping into place. He had it. It was all neatly placed in nice even rows, events at last making sense. Everything that had happened. The mysteries were all solved.

"It was you who hired Dick, wasn't it, Phan?. You had him kill Nicholas' wife."

"Yes. Her dead would take big insurance money away. He get nothing. I take it all away. His uncle was going to be next. But you get too close." Phan stuck the gun in JB's face again.

"So you had to have killed Dick. That day at the "Y". It was you."

"I had found him. I could get rid of him too."

"You hired him from the magazine, right? But you knew he was the same person who had been in Saigon when Song died. You must have kept track of him the same way you did Nicholas. So you paid him to destroy Nicholas. More than wily. Downright diabolical. I have to admit there is a certain panache to it all, Phan. An aligning of the proverbial stars. The men who were the cause of her death were the cause of their own. At least in your head. Very poetic, Phan. But it's still murder."

"So what? I owe those men nothing. My allegiance is to family. I take final revenge for Song."

During all of this conversation JB had been using the chisel he had hidden to cut at the duct tape binding his hands. Finally they were loose. He moved them to the front to get a grip on the seat of the chair.

While Phan stood in front of him contemplating his victory over Nicholas, savoring the revenge he had sought from his childhood onward, JB stood, bent forward with the chair and as quickly and as powerfully as he could slammed the heavy plywood back of the chair forward to smash onto Phan's head. The sound of wood cracking joined Phan's shriek of pain. He tried to pull up the gun in his hand to shoot at JB, but instead fired wildly. The shot roared and echoed in the warehouse, sailing off target and lodging in a wall.

The first blow of the chair JB wielded had stunned Phan and caused him to pull his arms up to his head. The second blow, quickly following the first—and because JB had bent to the side—came at him full on, smashing straight into Phan's face. That blow caused him to drop like a stone, out cold.

At the sound of the gunshot, there was a crash at the side door with a battering ram and a SWAT team of police officers came rushing in, shields up, guns aimmed, yelling and running, stomping around, feet echoing in the cavernous space. For seconds pure cacophony reigned. JB had sat the chair he was still taped to back down and was sitting, arms and legs crossed next to the passed out Nicholas. Phan was lying on the floor in front of him. The police circled them and pointed their rifles at them.

"Gee, I wish you'd called before you came. The place is such a mess and I didn't have time to clean. The one down there..." He pointed at Phan. "...is the reason you're here I guess."

Steve Kominski, the NYPD vice officer, came from behind the cops. "Stand down, men, and put that one in cuffs." He pointed at Phan. The officers relaxed their aim and went about their business. Steve went to JB and started to remove the duct tape from his chest. "You put together quite a party, don't you?"

"Once all the guests arrive it's a nicely symbiotic group, I think. Everybody giving everybody else a reason to be there. Speaking of which, why are you here?"

"Len called me. After your phone call to him he was worried. He said you'd got yourself into another mess and we needed to get you out of it?"

"But how did you find us?"

"He said you were in an old garage on Henry Street. There's not a lot of them."

"Well, Thank you."

"Happy to oblige. You want to explain all this?"

CHAPTER 18

It was almost four hours later when JB climbed out of a cab and headed for his apartment. He had spent the majority of that time with the police explaining all that he had found out about the Tok's and their involvement in the Mah-jongg Triad.

Immediately after Steve's rescue at the warehouse Phan had been arrested and taken to the local precinct for booking. Charges of racketeering and fraud first. Murder charges would be added later. Nicholas was attended to by para-medics then, still unconscious, was rushed to hospital with a major concussion from Phan's blow to his head.

JB had ridden with Steve back to his office to give his statement, then had gone to the hospital to check on Nicholas. His uncle, Sam, was already there. They had sat together until they could get an update on Nicholas' condition.

JB opened his apartment door and discovered Len sitting on his couch. He really did have to do something about all the extra keys to his place he had floating around.

Len stood. "You're here."

"Everybody's gotta be someplace," JB answered, quoting the old joke. He turned to hang up his jacket. Len was on him before he finished. They hugged.

"You're okay?"

"I'm fine."

Sitting on the couch JB began to explain to Len what had happened to him that day. "So it was Phan who had instigated this whole thing. His need for revenge on Nicholas for what he did to Song ended up pulling down the entire Triad organization."

"All over some girl."

"His sister, Len. Not really sufficient reason for his actions, but a bit more compelling."

"Still, just a girl. And a B-girl in a Vietnamese hustler bar at that."

"Who can understand that kind of passion, Len?"

"That's the kind of passion you usually rent by the hour." He leaned forward and picked up some papers from the coffee table. "While you were gone I was reading this." Len handed JB the pages he had torn from the back of Dick's Big Book the day he was killed by Phan.

"I had meant to read those myself, but the handwriting was practically indecipherable. And I got busy. What's in them?"

"It's what I thought. Dick was working on his personal inventory. The fourth step in the AA program. He confessed to his affair with Song."

"His affair? But she was Nicholas' girlfriend."

"Not according to those papers. Dick says he and Song were lovers. Nicholas was a jealous rival and that's what led to the fight at the bar the day of the explosion."

"So there's yet another version of this tale. Phan says that Nicholas killed his sister. Nicholas said that she was crushed…"

"And Dick says that she died in a fall. What's the truth?"

"I have a feeling we'll never know. What with both Phan and Dick out of the picture, and Nicholas in the condition he's in. I'm afraid we'll never get to the truth."

"What about Nicholas' condition?"

"At last report it doesn't look so good. He's regained consciousness but the blow Phan gave him has taken his memory again. He can remember up to when he was about twelve, after that its a complete blank. The doctor doesn't think any of it will come back this time. The brain can only take so many hits before it gives up completely."

"Then we'll never know what really happened."

"Yep. It is a *Rashomon*-esque sort of ending, isn't it?"

"Huh?"

"The Kurosawa film?"

"Oh, right."

"In which each of the observers of an event are able to produce substantially different but equally plausible accounts of the same event."

"Of course. I swear to God, JB, sometimes you're ten feet of pain in the ass stuck in a six foot sack..."

Saigon, Vietnam
1973

The Happy Club, located just off of Saigon's Tu Do Street, that early Sunday morning was silent and empty after a raucous night before. The growing sunlight from the street, filtered by the potted plants on the small streetside veranda, created lines of dust set swirling by the movement of a young boy shuffling around in the darkened club.

The boy was an eleven year old Phan Trang Tok, the first son of the owner of the nightclub. Next in the family was his sister, Song Le, the light in Phan's eye. For Phan this tiny angel, his older sister, had literally replaced his mother when she had died a few years before. Song had stepped up to take care of the whole Tok family. Behind Phan was his little brother, only seven, and a nuisance. Already he was becoming like their father, disapproving and censorious, never content with what they already had.

Phan was rummaging that morning among the discarded bottles of *Ba me Ba*—the local beer—crushed cigarettes, and other debris for any lost piasters or loose change that may have fallen from the pockets of the GI's that had crowded the bar the night before. Phan did this every morning before he started sweeping the place up. There were mornings when Phan had found big amounts, as much as a weeks wages from his job as the bar clean-up boy. Money just left or lost under a table. The Americans were so rich they just threw their money away. And what he found allowed him to make a few extra dollars, something all Vietnamese kids should learn to do at a very young age.

Phan's feet stepped through the flashing dots of white light from the mirrored disco ball that spun over the dance floor as he searched. A coin sparkled over by the bar, under the brass rail. He bent to retrieve it. That's when he heard a man's heavy footsteps going up the outside stairs at the side of the building. Must be an American, he thought. They always stomped and made noise when they went anywhere. Not like Vietnamese men, who padded more silently about.

❀❀❀

Nicholas Bonanno had finally gotten off guard duty that morning and, after taking a shower and shaving, had left his barracks and headed to The Happy Club to see his girl. He had met her at the bar a few weeks before and had to admit he had fallen hard for her. She was beautiful and sexy, especially when the spotlight caught her as she sang her rendition of *I Fall To Pieces* with the band that performed at the club. He stopped and picked up a bouquet of flowers from an old woman sitting on the curb. She nodded and smiled a gapped toothed grin made brown from the beetle nuts she chewed, thanking him for the few American coins he dropped in her palm. The mixture of colors in the flowers was sure to please Song's simple tastes. That was what he found so attractive about the Vietnamese girl. She was a sweet young woman, not at all hard or crass like the majority of the girls that worked in the clubs. The harshness of the enviroment hadn't yet jaded his sweet Song.

The bar was closed this early on a Sunday so Nicholas walked past the white *Citroën* parked on the street outside the club and went to the side of the building where he started to climb the stairs.

The stairs led to the family living quarters above the bar. Who could it be going up there? Phan wondered. This early? As he came down that morning he had seen Song lying asleep in her bed, naked, with a man. It was not an unusual sight for a young boy to see in war weary Saigon. All the girls that worked for his father slept with the men customers. For the money they paid. It was expected of them. His sister, as the owners child, wasn't expected to sell herself, but she supplemented the small amounts of money her father gave her with her own money, earned from liaisons with men who she called her benefactors. Phan was sure she wasn't really a whore, not like the sluts that shouted at passerby's a few streets over. Papa said they were trash; cheap, flashy tramps that would sell themselves for a few coins.

Song was different. She was the singer with the

band that played at the club. She had a soft growl in her small almost baby doll voice that perfectly suited the songs by the American Patsy Cline she sang so well, especially when she was amplified through the microphone. That she graciously accepted gifts and money from those men who wished to take care of her didn't make her a whore. It made her cherished and wanted. A finder of gold Popular.

Phan went to the front window and looked out at the street. It was beginning to be busy with people going about their morning business; going to church, looking for breakfast, street vendors setting up their booths against the curbs. The betting parlor next door, said to be connected with a gang of local gangsters, was already open. There had been an attack by a rival gang just the week before that completely wreaked the place. All the furniture smashed, paint cans splattered all over the walls. But it had been cleaned up and was already reopened. Such gang wars were always going on. Wars within wars. It was the way things were in Saigon.

A white older model French passenger car was parked between the bar and the parlor. Such ostentatious wealth in this neighborhood could only belong to gangsters, or to one of the ex-patriot French that still stayed in the city. Phan picked up his broom and began to sweep. His father would be down soon wanting to open up for the late morning crowd. Phan didn't want another ear cuffing because he hadn't cleaned up fast enough.

As he swept Phan could hear feet scuffling around upstairs. And there were two men shouting. What was going on? He stopped and looked up, listening, trying to decipher what was being said up there, but it was in English, and his English wasn't very good. The building was built of native materials, and insulation in Vietnam's tropical climate was unheard of, so he could make out from the tone that there was an argument going on. In Song's room at the front. The man who had climbed the stairs and her bed partner were fighting?

Upstairs, in Song's room, Nicholas Bonanno had just thrown the bouquet of sweet smelling flowers he had brought to give to his best girl at the wall. The strength with which he threw them caused the petals to fly in an explosion of colorful confetti that floated limply to the floor. Song was sitting up, the blanket that had barely covered her now held up to her breasts, but still showing the honey colored curve of her waist and buttocks. Fear filled her soft features at Nicholas' anger.

The other man, who had been asleep, also lying naked beside Song when Nicholas had burst in, was now sitting up on the side of the bed. He was facing Nicholas, who was screaming at them after discovering the two of them in their compromising circumstances.

"You fucking son of a bitch," Nicholas yelled. "You bastard. You low life. You motherfu…"

"Jesus, man, get a grip," Dick said. He ran a hand over his crew cut blond hair. His body, chiseled by the Beret training he had just completed, glistened in the soft light of the room. "So I slept with the whore. What did you expect? She's a primo piece, guy."

"I'll kill you, you bastard. I swear you're a dead man. She was mine. How could you…"

"She was available to the highest bidder, Nicky. What did you expect? That she was gonna be true to only you? You were fooling yourself."

"I love her, Dick. I only introduced you two because I trusted you. How long have you…"

"Everyday since we met." He reached for her hand. "She's a beauty, Nicky. I had to have her." In fact, he too had fallen in love with the girl, but his macho posturing couldn't let him admit it to Nicholas. It would be too much information given away.

Song scooted over and crouched under Dick's arm, mostly as protection from the obviously angry and raging Nicholas.

At this blatent gesture of Song's betrayal and unfaithfulness Nicholas moaned a drawn out, "Noooo. Damn it, Song, you can't be with him. You're mine." Nicholas growled and with his hands outthrust ran toward Dick, intending to choke him. To make him leave his girl alone. To get him away from her.

Song, on her hands and knees, jumped away from Dick to cower against the headboard of the bed, leaving Dick to fend off Nicholas' attack by himself. Nicholas shouted, "You can't have her, Dick. You've got to stay away from her..."

Dick stood from the bed and simply pushed hard at Nicholas' shoulders when he was close enough. Nicholas stumbled backward, then regained his balance to once again have a go at Dick. Who now was holding a military issue revolver on him. "Nicky, you stay back or I'll shoot. Don't think I won't."

❀❀❀❀

The white car parked between the front of the bar and the betting parlor was filled front seat and back with enough explosives to destroy a good couple of blocks of buildings.

The explosion itself was loud enough to be heard as far as the American Embassy a mile away. The *Citroën* had been purchased for cash from a down on his heels Frenchman the week before and placed there by the leader of the rival gang of the gambling den owner next door. For him it was payback for the accidental death of his wife and daughter three weeks before in a similar attack on his home. That he had ties to the Vietcong—who had supplied the explosives—was only a secondary consideration to the revenge being sought.

The blast completely obliterated the front of the bar, upstairs and down. The explosion blew the buildings materials back into the bar, creating a dense choking shower out of bits of concrete, glass, and disintegrated board. A whooshing heated surge of air caught Phan, who was still sweeping, and lifted him off the floor so he flew backward and was thrown over the bar. He landed crouched in a ball safely on the rubber mats that covered the flooring back there. His arms, wrapped over his head, protected him as the big mirror that hung on the back bar shattered and shards of it fell to the ground along with broken bottles and glassware.

Upstairs the entire wood floor, or the ceiling of the club, depending on your place in the building, was literially eaten away, as if a monstrous dog had taken a hungry bite out of it. A half circle landing of torn and splintered wood was left behind, the rest of the pulverized lumber falling below to become rubble on the ground of the club. The bed, still standing on its little bit of flooring, with Song still lying on it, remained tenaciously clinging to that bit of floor, one end hanging out over the exposed opening. The girl had been thrown backward and was sprawled across the plaster and debris covered sheets. She was out cold.

Both Nicholas and Dick had been driven to the ground by the end of a massive rafter beam that had held up the roof of the building. Its outer end had been torn from the blasted and crumbling concrete of the front wall and been stopped by crashing onto the remnant of floor by the door where the men were having their stand-off. Nicholas was on one side of the beam, Dick was on the other. Dick's gun had been torn from his hand and lay near the door.

As the men were coming back to conscienceness

there was a loud splintering sound. The part of the beam still connected to the building had finally cracked free and came crashing down, a battering ram that first slammed itself across the bed where Song was still lying. It stayed there for a moment crushing and compressing the bed under it, then the weight of it plus gravity pulled it so that it rolled off and landed as a bridge across the cavity where the floor had been.

Nicholas, standing but still dazed and disoriented, finally got his bearings and looked out over the damage to the house. He spotted Song still lying on the bed. He called to her, but she didn't react to his voice. She remained still, lying on the bed. Fear began to rise in him as he used the beam as a sort of tightrope and carefully made his way over the gapping hole out to the end of the bed still clinging to its bit of flooring. He leaned over and grabbed at Song's foot to pull her toward him.

As he did he realized why she was not moving. Pulling her to him his greatest fear was realized— Song was dead. The heavy falling beam had crushed her; breaking her bones, bursting her heart, killing her instantly. The same beam he was now standing on had been the weapon of destruction that had taken his girl away. He pulled her close to him and stood, holding her limp body to his chest. She felt almost weightless in his arms, as if her spirit had already left her, that it was only a shell he was holding so close to him. Tears stung his eyes as he started to crab step his way back to the safety of the narrow landing.

Fighting to keep his balance as he carried Song's

lifeless body on the beam, Nicholas saw Dick standing on the landing, watching him. Dick was still naked, his body pasted with white plaster dust, streaked from the sweat rolling off his skin. His eyes were dark holes of anger staring from the pale plaster mask covering his face. He stood there, grim, seething, breathing hard, holding the gun at his side, glaring at Nicholas, cuddling his girl. His Song.

He raised his arm. "If I can't have her." He aimmed the gun in Nicholas' direction. "Then you can't either." He fired. The dust in his eyes threw off his aim and the bullet went low, not hitting the intended target. Nicholas' head or heart wasn't hit. Instead the bullet slashed into Nicholas' leg, causing him to shout out in pain and rear back, losing his already precarious balance on the beam. He dropped to his knee. Blood poured from the roughly opened wound in his leg, soaking his pants in the red warm sticky liquid. The weight of Song's body suddenly shifted in his arms and she rolled away from him.

Trying to keep hold of her Nicholas grabbed her arm, gripping it tightly. She was now hanging off the beam, her dead weight straining every muscle in Nicholas' arm. He felt her begin to slip from his grip. He tried to use his other arm to give him more leverage, but her arm continued to slip through his hands. His grip wasn't strong enough to hold on to her. She fell away and landed with a crash into the rubble on the floor below. Nicholas, without Song's weight to keep him upright, had fallen himself and he was now hanging off the beam. His chest pressed against the beam, his arms trying to hold on to the massive block of wood.

Dick, after firing the gun had discarded it and started to walk the beam toward Nicholas' hanging body. He finally reached him and grinned down at him, his face a mask of hate and evil. "Why don't you join her, Nicky," he rasped. He raised his bare foot and stomped on Nicholas's arm putting all his weight behind his leg. Nicholas yelled in pain. Then Dick's foot stomped him again. And again. Dick kicked and pushed at Nicholas with his bare feet until Nicholas had no choice but to let loose of the beam and fall himself.

He landed close to Song's body. As he started to lose conscienceness he saw Phan, her little brother, standing over her body, crying.

It was at that moment that Phan vowed revenge on Nicholas. At that moment he began to form the plan that would bring his sister's killer down. He would destroy him.

Soon enough Phan began to gather information on Nicholas, haunting his barracks, asking questions, finding out anything and everything he could about the American. Soon enough he began to press his father to make a move to America.

Dick had made his way back to the landing, got dressed, and left the shell of a building by the still intact side stairs. He rejoined his outfit and spent the next years in the jungle's of Southeast Asia fighting, killing, drinking to forget that horrendous morning, carrying a torch for the girl he had lost in the blast.

Nicholas was found by the MP's that had responded to the blast and was carried out of the building, taken to a Army hospital, and finally, awarded a Purple Heart and sent back to his hometown, Yonkers, NY.

About the author

Ken Lansdowne has lived in California, Nevada, New York City, New Mexico, and now lives in Denver Colorado.

The first novel in *The Bent Mystery* series is *Secrets Don't Belong In Closets*, the beginning. Second is *A Murderous Ball of Fluff. The Fairy Dust Killer* is the third. Fourth is *Home Sweet HoMo*. Fifth is *Dance: Ten Murder:Maybe?.* Sixth is *A Mystery, Wrapped In A Mystery, Surrounded By A Mystery.* Seventh is *The Art Of Death,* and number eight is *Bathhouse Bloodbath!*

There is also a Gay themed Christmas novella: *Jacob Marley*

If you would like to get an automatic e-mail when the next book in the series is ready for release sign up at k.lansd@outlook.com. Simply put the word "LIST" in the subject line of your email. Your e-mail address will never be shared and you can unsubscribe at any time.

Word-of-mouth is crucial for any author to succeed. If you enjoyed the book please consider leaving an online review, even if it is only a line or two: it would make all the difference and would be very much appreciated. If you didn't like it I apologize for taking up your time: my purpose was only to entertain or give you a laugh or two.

www.ingramcontent.com/pod-product-compliance
Lightning Source LLC
Chambersburg PA
CBHW070833120626
46556CB00002B/743